CRUEL STORIES

ISBN: 978-1-957121-34-5

All Text © 1978 -2022 by Donald Tyson

Editor and Publisher, Joe Morey

Cover art © 2022 by K.L. Turner
Cover and interior design by Cyrusfiction Productions

Weird House Press
Central Point, OR 97502
www.weirdhousepress.com

CRUEL STORIES

DONALD TYSON

WEIRD HOUSE

TABLE OF CONTENTS

INTRODUCTION

The *conte cruel* or cruel story is a genre of fiction defined by French writers of the late 19th century. Its nominal point of origin is usually fixed on the 1883 collection of horror stories by Comte de Phillipe August Villiers de l'Isle-Adam (1838 – 1889), which he titled *Contes Cruels* (*Cruel Stories*). However, earlier collections of stories by other authors also fit into the parameters of the genre, notable among them *Tales of the Grotesque and Arabesque* by Edgar Allan Poe, which was published in 1840.

What characterizes the genre is a tendency to avoid supernatural horror, and adhere to the horror of man against man or the horror of self-inflicted circumstance, both of which can give rise to irony and exquisite frustration. The famous statement by Jean-Paul Sartre, "Hell is other people," very much applies to this genre, where suffering is inflicted by one flawed individual upon another, although sometimes the imperfect individual inflicts it upon himself through foolishness or hubris.

The horror of the *conte cruel* is often quite visceral in nature, involving torture, mutilation, and blood, or at least the foreshadowing of these things. There is frequently a sexual element at play, an erotic subtext that gives intense energy to the horrifying circumstance of the protagonist or his victim. In his 1927 essay *Supernatural Horror In Literature*, H. P. Lovecraft observed about the genre, "the wrenching of the emotions is accomplished through dramatic tantalizations, frustrations, and gruesome physical horrors." In the *conte cruel* there is always a twist applied to the knife as it is going in.

H. P. Lovecraft believed in an impersonal universe, that humanity was treated no better and no worse than all other forms of life. His Old Ones look upon our race with indifference. But what if the universe is not indifferent to our suffering? What if there exists a special malice that is reserved for humankind due to our special place in the order of life? We, more than any other animal species, are equipped to experience horror to its fullest degree. Our superior intelligence allows us to imagine horrors that are beyond the conception of lesser species. We are capable of suffering that goes beyond mere physical pain and distress. We can suffer in the mind as well as in the body, and where a capacity exists in Nature, then surely there also exists an agency to fill it. We have the ability to experience cruelty to a greater degree than any other living thing, and since Nature abhors a vacuum, it may be that a dispenser of cruelty has been created just for us, to allow us to utilize our unique capacity to feel horror.

The thematic link which the *conte cruel* genre of horror fiction shares with the *Grand Guignol* tradition of French theater should be obvious. Both arose from the decadence of the late 19th century that inflamed the Anarchist movement in Europe and sparked the famous declaration "God is dead" by Friedrich Nietzsche, although the roots of a taste for torture and blood in popular entertainment lie deeper amid the atheism and nihilism of the 19th century. In the *Théâtre du Grand-Guignol*, founded at Paris in 1897, audiences could watch actors tortured on the rack, branded with red-hot irons, blinded, disfigured, stabbed, shot, decapitated, eviscerated, all with realistic spurting blood. Essentially, these plays were the dramatization of *contes cruels*.

The present collection of stories was written over the span of four and a half decades. Some of them are among my earliest works of horror fiction. "Going to See Mr. Winters" was the first-prize winner of a Mount Saint Vincent University literary contest that I won at the age of 24. The story went on to win a prize in the 1978 Nova Scotia Writing Competition, hosted by the Writers' Federation of Nova Scotia, and it was published in the Fall-1978 issue of *Alpha*, the student union magazine of Acadia University. It was my statement concerning the growing hopelessness and despair I observed in Western society, which was evident even in the mid-1970s. Of course it is much worse today. To my complete disgust, the university magazine in which the story was published placed the entire story on one page with the exception of the final sentence, which was buried by itself in the back of the magazine. This destroyed the effectiveness of the story, since most readers either would not have bothered to turn to the final line, or would not have been able to find it.

"The Glen of the Green Women" was inspired by a few lines in a poem by English poet Sir Walter Scott, and by the Scottish legend behind the poem. The style of the story is intended to suggest its medieval setting. It was published in *Black Cat Mystery Magazine* (vol. 1, issue no. 3) in 1981. I've rewritten the ending of the story to heighten its dramatic effect. This is quite a common practice for me. When I look over an older story I haven't looked at in years, I frequently see small ways to improve it, or sometimes large ways.

"Cruising" is an unusual story for me due to its length. It is what is known as a short-short, a story of only a few hundred words. I am much more comfortable as a writer with medium-length and long stories because they give me a chance to set mood, evolve character and tell a story. The short-short relies on a surprise twist at the end. I've never had much success with this form, but "Cruising" came to me one afternoon without effort. I remember that I wrote it in longhand with a fountain pen while kneeling at the side of my bed, using my bed as a desk. The machine gun style is not my usual style, but seems to work for this story. It was published in *Twilight Zone Magazine*, September 1982 issue, and subsequently reprinted in the paperback anthology *Night Cry* (Summer, 1985).

These stories, and others that have never been published, such as "False Image" and "Janus," were written during the first phase of my writing career, when I was trying to establish myself as a professional fiction writer and playwright. At a certain point it became obvious to me that if I wished to make a living, I would have to shift my focus from fiction to nonfiction. This explains the rather long gap between my earlier stories and my more recent efforts, which were produced when I came to the equally life-changing determination that if I wished to make any kind of mark as a fiction writer, I had better not let any more time go by, or I would be dead from old age.

I have a definite fondness for some of the stories in this collection. This is usually deadly for a writer, because we have no ability to look at our own work with the detachment necessary to evaluate its worth. I hope I haven't put the jinx on these stories by admitting that I like them.

None the less, I will mention "The Nail," which was published in *Weird*

Fiction Review (Fall, 2014). To me it seems to be an almost perfect story. I mean that in a structural sense. I was able to accomplish almost exactly what I set out to do, which is seldom true for a writer. Most of the time we chase our inspiration through thickets and over fences. "The Nail" came forth fully formed, like Athena from the forehead of Zeus.

"Fingernails" revolves around a very special gift a loving husband gives to his equally loving wife. The motif of a gift given with fatal consequences is common throughout horror fiction, but the concept behind this particular gift, which is by no means beyond the bounds of possibility, intrigued me. The evil countess mentioned in the story is an historical figure. Relics of dead saints have always been supposed by the Church of Rome to carry esoteric power, so why not the relic of a particularly evil sinner?

The extremities of love form the underlying theme for "The Ivory Box," which is set in the Forbidden City of ancient China. It illustrates how love, when pressed too hard, distorts and becomes destructive, its consequences indistinguishable from hate. This is one of the few stories in the collection with an overtly supernatural aspect, although many of them have an underlying otherness that exists off stage, as it were.

"What Is Happening" illustrates how complacency and wishful thinking can become a kind of man-trap that we set for ourselves, then forget about and walk into. There is an absurd element to this story, but it is no less horrifying because of it. The title is both a question and a statement. Sometimes the chains we forge for ourselves can be impossible to break, and establish our fate long before we have any intimation that something is amiss.

"Tongue of the Bell" concerns an artist who is suddenly presented with the perfect method for murdering his domineering, wealthy wife. He learns that every action, no matter how trivial it seems, has consequences which may, under the right conditions, be of critical importance. Unfortunately he acquires this bit of wisdom too late for it to be of service.

"The Rose Circle" is a novella of pure Gothic horror set in the latter half of the 19th century, which I wrote specifically for this collection. It tells the story of how an impressionable young woman of good family can so easily fall into the net cast by an unscrupulous but charismatic spiritual leader. It is a tale old as time and modern as today, as the newspaper accounts of Charles Manson's Family certify. But it might as easily have been Aleister Crowley's cult of Thelema in Sicily, or the Peoples Temple of the Reverend Jim Jones in Guyana. All such cults are driven by the same social dynamic.

A few of the stories were written in a single evening and then put away for decades without being re-read. This is true of "Found Art," a tale about a rescue at sea that is not so altruistic as it first appears. "Future Indefinite" amazed me when I re-read it for the first time since writing it years ago. I had put it away as a first draft without even bothering to correct its spelling errors. I do not remember writing it, and assume I was in a kind of trance state when I did so, which sometimes happens when I write fiction.

"Dream A Little Dream of Me" is a more recent story. I wrote it, and did not know when to stop writing it. I ended up with a beginning that I liked, but the second half of the story dragged. Recently I cut the second half off, threw it away, and wrote a new briefer conclusion, keeping the first half of the story more or less in its original form. The result is a great improvement over the original version, in my opinion.

I like to infuse my stories with historical accuracies, a little trick I learned by studying the work of H. P. Lovecraft, who would mingle real books with books from his own imagination, actual places and events with places and events completely fictional. "A Leaf from the Cottonian Genesis" is an example of this mingling of the real with the unreal. The illuminated manuscript of the Book of Genesis described in the story did exist, and formed a part of the famed Cottonian Library, until it was largely destroyed in a fire, leaving only fragments remaining.

Another example of blending fiction with nonfiction occurs in "The Seed of Vass" which takes place in part in Salem Village right around the time of the infamous witch trials, which began in 1692. The various names and places mentioned are historical. Even the names of the characters are drawn from the list of residents in Salem Village at the time.

"False Image" has never before been published. I did, however, submit it to a number of magazines at some point in the mid-1980s. All the editors rejected the story as not suitable for their markets. One was kind enough to write me a personal letter, in which he stated that it was the most effective example of the *conte cruel* that he had ever read. Prior to this, I had never encountered the term. This letter, which I never forgot, was the seminal spark for the present story collection and the source of its title.

FINGERNAILS

"If you were going to make the perfect backscratcher, what would be the ideal thing to make it from?"

Angela was accustomed to her husband's mental gymnastics. He had been born under the sign of Capricorn, and true to the nature of the energetic mountain goat, his mind liked to leap from one oddity to another with no connecting bridge to lend coherence to his utterances.

"I don't know – plastic, probably. Everything is made from plastic these days."

"Try again," Toby told her with his boyish smile.

They lounged on opposite ends of their living room couch, wine glasses in their hands. It was the comfortable hour of evening that lay midway between returning from their jobs in the city and getting ready for bed. They had dined on baked salmon, showered, and put on robes. A low fire glowered on the iron grate in the fireplace. Scrabble tiles lay scattered over the top of the glass coffee table. Both enjoyed board games that engaged the mind.

"Something organic? Teak, perhaps? Ebony? Rosewood?"

"All good materials that have been used since ancient times, but not the best material."

They sat in silence and sipped their wine.

"Well I really don't know, Toby. Are you going to tell me or not?"

He sat upright and set his wine glass on the edge of the coffee table.

"The best thing to make a back scratcher from would be human fingernails, of course. What else in the entire world is specifically designed to scratch human skin?"

She shuddered involuntarily.

"That's just, *ugh*, what an unpleasant idea."

"I'm sorry to hear you say that," he said, still smiling. "Your birthday is tomorrow, and you've been angling to trick me into telling what I bought for you."

She looked at him uncertainly. It was difficult sometimes to know if he was joking or serious.

"I suppose I can wait until tomorrow."

"You don't need to."

He sprang up and went to the entrance hall. Opening the drawer of a side table, he took from it a long box elegantly gift wrapped in forest green gift paper with silver lines running through it. Returning to the living room, he laid it gently on her outstretched hands.

"With love, from your better half. May you enjoy another year of happiness."

Her fingers trembled as she tore the paper off the box. He was such a tease. Could it be the pearl necklace she had admired at Tiffany's? She removed the lid.

It was a backscratcher. Her heart sank as she studied it, trying not to let her disappointment show. It was obviously an antique. The shaft and clutching hand were made of yellowed ivory that was beautifully carved. The hand, which possessed five fingers, was disturbingly similar to a human hand in shape, but somewhat smaller than life-sized. Indeed, as she looked at it, she realized that it was a woman's hand. The old ivory that constituted the palm and fingers had been carved with lines so cunningly that the hand resembled living flesh.

On the end of each curved finger was a yellowed fingernail that projected beyond the tip of the finger half an inch or so. These were not ivory. She looked closer, then could not conceal her sudden disgust as she drew back.

"Are they real?"

He laughed, enjoying the play of emotions across her face.

"Very real, and very human. Or so the elderly Romanian gentleman who sold it to me claims."

She laughed in disbelief, staring at him.

"But you can't expect me to use this? It's ... it's —" She searched for the right word. "It's ghoulish."

He raised a finger.

"Don't be too quick to judge until you've tried it."

"I'm not going to try it. You have to take it back."

"No return, no refund," he said. "The old gypsy was quite clear on that point."

"Then you keep it. I don't want it."

She let the backscratcher drop to the glass top of the table with a clatter.

"Now you're being childish," he said. "After I went through all the trouble of picking it out for you, the least you can do is try it once."

She pouted at him.

"It wasn't cheap, you know."

Her eyes wandered to the yellow fingernails at the ends of the ivory fingers. Each was beautifully manicured, but they were so long, they reminded her of the talons of a hawk. They seemed to be intact all the way down to where they entered into slots in the ivory, as though growing from it. Was it possible they has been torn out at the roots from some poor woman's hand?

"I really don't want to ..."

"Humor me."

Very well, she thought. Let him have his way. When he sees that I don't care for the ugly thing, he'll stop pestering me about it.

Turning on the couch, she opened the sash at the waist of her white silk robe and let its collar fall from her shoulders and arms, exposing her back down to the curves of her buttocks. She heard him pick up the backscratcher from the coffee table.

The fire had died down, and the air felt cool against her exposed skin.

"When are you going to –"

Something touched her between her shoulder blades. She gasped with pleasure. With excruciating slowness, the touch was drawn down her spine. She started to laugh, but it turned into a moan of delight. Her nipples became little spikes, and the muscles across her belly rippled. Her entire body from the roots of her hair to her toes tingled with sensation so intense, it was almost pain. Between her thighs she felt her labia flushing and expanding with hot blood.

"Nothing like a good scratch," her husband said, withdrawing the ivory hand.

She closed her eyes, licked her lips and drew her robe back over her shoulders, pressing hard on her nipples as she closed it in front. They still ached with desire.

"Did you try it?"

"I had no choice. The old man insisted I try it out before he would sell it to me."

Turning to him, she saw that his clear blue eyes had turned misty with barely suppressed passion.

"Of course I didn't take off my shirt. I can only imagine what it feels like on your bare skin."

"It feels ..."

She stopped, at a loss for words. They both stood up and went into the master bedroom, where they could play with their new toy.

After several hours, they found themselves too exhausted to continue. Angela set the backscratcher on her bedside table and lay beside her husband, who drew the sheet over her breasts. The bedroom was dark apart from the rectangle of light that shone in from the hallway.

"Did the old Romanian who sold it to you say where it came from?"

"He gave me a fairy story but I didn't believe him."

"Why not?"

"It was too incredible."

"Tell me."

He rolled onto his shoulder so that he could look at her face.

"He said the fingernails came from the hand of a famous Hungarian countess who was the wife of a great warrior who fought off the armies of the Ottoman Turks."

"What was her name?"

"Bathory, I think. Something like that."

The name held no meaning for her.

"How did this Countess Bathory lose her fingernails?"

"That's where the story gets absurd," he said. "According to the old man, she was an evil witch who liked to bathe in the blood of young girls to preserve her beauty."

"Sounds like some kind of vampire."

"She would hang the girls upside down by their heels, cut their throats, and wash herself in the hot blood that spurted from their necks."

Angela felt herself becoming aroused. The cool fabric of the sheet where it rested between her thighs tickled her. She frowned in the darkness and tried to ignore the feeling.

"How long did this go on?"

"Longer than you might expect. Years. Eventually she was discovered and convicted of witchcraft. Because she was a countess and her husband held so much power and wealth, she could not be executed. Instead, the authorities walled her up in a little room in her castle, with only a slot remaining open through which her keepers could pass her food and water. She lived for years in this dark prison and lost all her beauty. When she died, the wall was broken open and she was found to be a hideous old hag."

"What about the fingernails?"

"The old man said that before she was buried, one of gypsy witches who had helped her commit her murders tore out all the fingernails from her right hand and took them away with her. A search was made for the old woman, but she vanished into thin air and was never seen again."

"That's quite a story."

"A tall tale if ever there was one."

The silence lengthened between them. She heard the familiar sound of her husband's soft snores and knew he had fallen asleep.

She found herself in a windowless chamber with stone walls that were dimly illuminated by two flickering oil lamps that hung from brackets on chains. The chamber had a vaulted ceiling. A naked girl was suspended upside down by her feet from a pulley in the vault, her hands bound behind her back at her waist. Her long, blonde hair hung down like a shock of ripe wheat and almost brushed the rim of a wooden bucket that rested on the flagstones beneath her. The girl was weeping silently. Tears from the corners of her grey eyes trickled over her temples.

When the girl saw Angela approach, she began to writhe her body and plead for her life. It was not English but Angela understood her words.

"This one's a pretty one," she heard herself say in a voice deeper and more resonant than her own voice.

A naked old woman with long, grey hair and sagging breasts cackled and nodded. Angela realized with a slight shock that she also was naked.

Sudden anger flared in her heart. She slapped the blubbering girl hard across the face.

"Shut up, little fool."

Terrified, the girl became silent.

"You have lovely skin."

Angela raised her hand, and saw that her fingernails were longer than she usually kept them. Slowly, lovingly, she raked her hand down the girl's body from her blonde pubes to her breasts. Where her fingernails cut the skin, crimson rivulets of blood began to bead and run.

"Give me the knife," she heard herself say above the screams of the inverted girl.

Her shuddering sexual climax cast her out of the nightmare. She found herself seated on the padded bench in front of her makeup table. A mist of sweat chilled her naked body. From the bed she heard the snores of her husband, still deep in sleep.

She realized that she held the backscratcher. Hesitantly, she raised it over her shoulder and let its ivory hand touch her skin. The points of the nails caused her to groan involuntarily with pleasure. She began to draw it gently up and down her back.

Waves of orgasm washed over her and left her weak, with her heart hammering inside her chest. She had never in her life imagined there could be such physical ecstasy. Her ragged breaths hissed and trembled in her throat as she fought to control herself.

Glancing into the oval mirror above the table, she saw standing behind her a beautiful woman with coils of raven-black hair hanging around her graceful white neck. She wore a green silk dress with puffed sleeves and spreading skirts. The woman gazed out from the mirror as though aware she was being watched, all the while never ceasing to scratch Angela's back with her long fingernails.

"Angie? What are you doing? Come back to bed."

When her husband received no answer, he threw back the sheet and went over to where she sat. By the dim light that shone through the partly open bedroom door, he saw that her back was covered with streaks of blood. She continued to draw the backscratcher up and down as though in some kind of trance.

"Let me have that. You're hurting yourself."

He grabbed for the backscratcher, but quick as a cat she jumped to her feet and stepped away.

"Give it to me, darling. You're all covered with blood."

He moved toward her with his hand extended. She swung the backscratcher under his chin in an arc, and the long, sharp fingernails cut his throat.

Staggering back, he clutched his neck and stared at her with amazed eyes. The blood continued to spurt between his fingers in spite of his tight grip. Groping to find the foot of the bed with his other hand, he dropped to one knee.

She pushed him hard in the chest so that he fell on his back, and straddled his bare hips. His eyes blinked several more times with the wonder of a child, then stared at her in eternal incomprehension. With her free hand she dipped her fingers in the warm blood on his throat and voluptuously painted her cheeks and lips, tasting its coppery tang on the tip of her tongue.

All this while, she never ceased drawing the backscratcher up and down her bleeding back. She continued in this way hour after hour, until the scratches became deep slashes, and the muscles of her back were torn away; until the whiteness of her spine and ribs were exposed. Yet still she continued to scratch, scratch, scratch.

FOUND ART

When he saw the light, Harold Sims continued to sit with warm salt water lapping about his bare knees. He had already given up hope. The main pump was down – no electricity. Blisters from the emergency pump covered his soft palms. It lay somewhere abandoned under the waves that washed over the deck of his single-masted sailboat, the *Ellie II*.

Squalls hit without warning this time of year off the Florida Keys. The wind had rent the sail, swamped the boat and killed the power all in a single moment. In the dark hours of calm that followed he began to realize that despite his futile efforts to bail the hull it had also deprived him of his life.

After an indeterminate limbo the beam of a searchlight passed over him, then fixed on his face. A voice hailed. He looked around and noticed the illuminated profile of a ship. Weakly he pushed himself to his feet and caught the line that was cast down. With fatigue-stiffened fingers he looped it around his chest and felt himself lifted into the air even as the water-logged hull slipped under the gentle waves.

Still in a dreaming trance, Sims was helped over the rail of the ship and surrounded by a ring of smiling, sympathetic faces, none of them more than half his own age. The women carried champagne glasses. The men wore formal evening clothes. Colored party lights played over their hands as they unwrapped the line. A loud rock-and-roll beat throbbed in the air. Someone pressed a glass into his hand. He drank from it gratefully, wishing it were water instead of wine. It had a bitter flavor.

A slender young man in a white suit motioned the others aside with a proprietary gesture. He inspected Sims with alert dark eyes and patted him in a patronizing way on the cheek.

"Are you all right, my friend? You had a close call."

The voice was cultured, the accent foreign. It had that nasal New York twang that some Europeans put into their English in an effort to sound more American.

Sims shuddered. He opened his mouth to explain about the squall and the pump but the words caught in his throat.

"Don't try to talk now," the other said. "You are safe here on my yacht. I see that you are tired and need rest."

"Rest, yes," Sims repeated mechanically.

Suddenly he felt more weary than he had ever been in his life. Fatigue toxins that had accumulated in his blood during the long hours spent battling the rising water in the wreck were taking their toll. He could barely keep his salt-swollen eyes open.

Blinking owlishly, he tried to focus on his host. The man in white looked vaguely familiar. His narrow, swarthy face reminded Sims of that crazy millionaire Italian artist, what was his name, who jetted around the world putting on grandiose displays of performance art for the television cameras. Once he had wrapped the great pyramid in red plastic and staged a mock mass human sacrifice under the gaze of the sphinx. Sims had never paid much attention. It was not his idea of art.

"Your Dios Fablio," he said suddenly.

"Please, just Fablio. That is what my friends call me, and I want you to be my friend, Mr. – ?"

"Harold Sims. I'm an accountant from Miami. I was trying to sail to Jamaica when the squall …"

Sims tried to explain that he was on vacation, and had been taking the sailboat to Jamaica to join his wife, Ellie, and his daughter, Ann, who had flown to the island ahead of him. Instead he let go of the slim cool fingers of the Italian and trailed off into silence. For some reason his mind would not work properly. He longed to close his eyes and sleep. Dimly he heard Fablio talking. What was he saying? Sims made an effort to concentrate.

" – your coming is most fortuitous, Mr. Sims. No, no, do not try to thank me, I understand how you feel. To me, it is very clear. Your life has been spared in the service of art. You are the instrument and I am the craftsman. Together we will astound the world, I assure you."

There were curious lapses in Sims' awareness. He had a vague sense of dancing. The next thing he knew, a young woman with long golden hair and prominent breasts was leading him away from the circle of smiling faces toward a door. Behind him he heard laughter, and the voice of Fablio rising above it.

"He is my found art. So naive, so gauche, so utterly middle-class."

Sims awoke in a strange bed. Pale moonlight filtered through the slats of the blinds over the windows. He felt the gentle motion of waves and realized that he was still on Fablio's yacht.

Someone had taken off his flowered shirt and Bermuda shorts while he was unconscious and dressed him in blue silk pajamas that did not quite fit his stomach bulge. The night was silent. He licked cracked lips with a dry tongue and made a wry face at the unpleasant metallic taste in his mouth. There was no way of knowing if he had slept for a few hours or around the clock.

He rolled over and became aware of a vague shape lying beside him under the silk sheet. Remembering the stunning blonde who had led him to the cabin, he smiled and reached out.

The furious explosion of motion when he touched the pale shoulder paralyzed him with surprise. At first he thought a leopard clawed and struck and snapped its teeth in his face. For several seconds he struggled to hold it off. Dimly he realized the wiry body belonged to a man. With a grunt of effort he threw his attacker from the bed and heard him strike the floor and scramble away. A door slammed.

At the same moment Sims was on his feet on the other side of the bed looking around in the gloom for some weapon he could use to defend himself. Nothing presented itself. He held his breath and listened, heart thundering under his ribs.

Cautiously he rounded the bed. There was enough light to show the empty floor. He peered into the corners of the cabin without seeing any threatening shadows. Drawing a shuddering breath, he straightened up and padded on bare feet to the door. Here he paused with his ear against the panel. When he again heard nothing he tried to open the door.

Locked. He felt around the walls on either side of the frame for a light switch. Wherever it was, he could not locate it. There was no lamp beside the bed. Tentatively he banged his fist against the door. When no response came he pounded harder.

"Can anyone hear me? Hello? I'm locked in! I've been attacked! Hello?"

He kept this up for several minutes, then stopped with a curse. The door was solid teak. It did not even yield when he tried his shoulder against it. In frustration he rattled the brass handle.

"Probably all dead drunk," he muttered. "The one who came at me must have been on drugs."

He searched the cabin by touch for something to pry at the handle, but without success. The windows were locked by key and made of inch-thick shatterproof glass to resist the pounding of waves during storms.

Sims shrugged. Maybe the crazy bastard who had attacked him had done him a favor by slamming the door when he bolted out of the cabin. It must have locked automatically when it shut. At least he was on the other side. As an added defense he took the wooden chair that sat beside the door and wedged its straight back firmly under the handle.

After a while Sims went back to the bed and lay down on it. There seemed nothing else to do until morning stirred the other passengers out of their drunken stupors. He did not mean to sleep, but was still worn out from the ordeal of the storm. His eyes drooped shut. His breaths lengthened.

❧

It was still dark when he awoke. The night seemed endless. Yawning, he rolled onto his side and scratched himself between the shoulder blades. He continued to lie there, eyes moving around the shadowy corners of the cabin with restless unease.

There seemed no reason to be nervous. The yacht was silent. From where he lay on the edge of the mattress he could see in the moonlight the locked door. The chair was still in place. For some reason he found himself lying perfectly still and breathing shallow breaths through parted lips, straining his ears for the slightest whisper. This went on so long that at last he forced himself to take a normal breath and consciously relaxed his tense muscles.

In a band of moonlight beside his shoulder the silk sheet domed to a small point and lifted away from the mattress. Sims stared at the little moving bump with disgust. A bedbug. Of all the myriad kinds of pests, he hated bedbugs the most. They invaded the security of the bed while a man lay helpless in sleep, like little blood-sucking vampires.

He continued to lie watching it move in tentative arcs under the sheet. Idly he wondered if he should try to kill it or just resign himself to sleeping in the chair. The dome of silk pressed higher. The bug must be standing on its hind legs, Sims thought. Still it rose, until it was a miniature peak under the sheet. Sims' eyes widened.

In the perfect silence the ripping of the silk made a soft hiss. A narrow spike of gleaming steel extended out through the hole into the moonlight. Here it paused, as if blindly sensing its surroundings. It was some kind of giant needle, Sims realized, impossibly long. He watched in fascination as it withdrew itself and vanished, leaving only a pinhole in the sheet to mark its passage.

Acute terror snapped some bond of restraint inside his brain. He bellowed with rage as he scrambled to his feet and blindly reached under the bed to drag out the man that lay hidden there. They grappled, wrestling and striking wildly. Sims fought like a possessed animal. Somehow his hands found their way around the skinny neck of his smaller foe and he forced the man back across the bed, throttling him, not even conscious of the fingernails that raked his forearms.

The moonlight fell across his attacker's face. It was Fablio. Recognition of his identity brought back a shadow of sanity to Sims. He loosened his grip, and the Italian coughed and gasped for breath.

"Kill me, yes, why don't you kill me?" he whispered, laughing softly. "Sacrifice my life in the service of my art. I will make you famous."

The insane shadows that danced in the rolling eyes of the artist diverted Sims' rage into a less lethal channel. Instead of returning his fingers to Fablio's neck, Sims struck him repeatedly in the face with his fist until the Italian went limp.

He straightened from the body in disgust, his stomach heaving. Violence always made him sick. Pain throbbed through his right hand from his lacerated knuckles.

"Crazy bastard," he gasped in reproach, staring down at the limp human shape. "You goddamned crazy bastard."

He took the chair from under the handle of the door and swung it against the panel repeatedly, yelling for help at the top of his lungs. After a dozen thuds the chair fell apart in his hands. Breathing heavily, he leaned against the door and listened. There was no sound from the other side, not even the sound of the yacht's diesel engine, he realized for the first time. That was not right.

Something gleamed on the floor. The needle. Sims picked it up to examine it, and discovered that it was really an elongated ice pick with a wooden handle. At least it was something he could use to defend himself.

He returned to the bed and carefully felt in all the pockets of the unconscious Italian. In the left side of the pants he found a ring of keys. Hardly daring to hope, Sims tried them one after the other in the lock of the door. At the third key the lock turned. With the ice pick held in front of him, he stepped cautiously into the deserted corridor. He paused to re-lock the door. The last thing he wanted was the mad artist creeping behind him through the darkness.

Electricity was out all over the yacht. Sims felt his way from cabin to cabin, calling loudly for help. The entire vessel seemed deserted. He found his way outside onto the deck. Colorless pre-dawn light glowed on the eastern horizon. The yacht was out of sight of land. He made a complete search and discovered one of the emergency lifeboats missing from its cradle. That explained where the others had gone but not the reason for their departure.

Nothing made any sense. He began to suspect that he was the butt of some elaborate practical joke. Soon the guests and crew of the yacht would jump out from wherever they were hiding and laugh. Only there was no where for them to hide. He became more convinced of this fact as he continued to search the yacht. He located the radio room, meaning to call the coast guard for assistance. To his dismay the radio was smashed. Gradually it came home to Sims that he was adrift on a ghost ship, alone except for the madman who had tried to murder him.

Or had Fablio really been trying to kill him?

There was nothing to do but wait for rescue. Sooner or later someone would notice the drifting yacht. He was in no danger if the weather remained calm. There was plenty of food and water – Sims checked on this to make certain the mad Italian had not dumped these stores overboard. He possessed the keys to the cabins and the only serious weapon apart from the knives in the galley, the door to which he carefully locked.

Sims searched around until he found a coil of fine nylon line and dragged an ornately carved wooden arm chair from one of the deserted cabins into the corridor, then unlocked the door to his own cabin and pulled the chair in behind him. The strengthening morning light showed Fablio sprawled across the bed. He approached to see if the Italian was still alive. The unconscious man blew shallow puffs of air through his swollen nose and bloody lips. Sims prodded him, half convinced he was faking it. The Italian did not respond. When he realized Fablio really was out cold, Sims muscled the artist's limp body into the chair, tying his feet to the legs and securing his wrists together behind the back. Fablio might be able to rock the chair onto its side but he was not going anywhere.

He sat on the bed with his knees drawn up cross-legged, head resting back on the headboard and the ice pick across his lap. For a while he watched the lolling head of the Italian, expecting it to rise up at any moment and dreading the expression he might see on that narrow, dark face. When Fablio awoke, he would damn well find out what was going on, Sims told himself. Then he might or might not press charges. He owed the Italian something for rescuing him.

His mind drifted. Imperceptibly he slid into a profound sleep. He was still exhausted and had not gained more than a couple of hours sleep since being rescued – not enough to restore his strength.

Full daylight blazed through the blinds when he opened his eyes for the third time. Fablio stood at the foot of the bed rubbing his wrists and staring down at him with a mild expression. Two uniformed men stood at his sides. Sims flinched and groped for the ice pick, then saw that one of the men held it in a small pair of pliers and was examining it.

"It's blood all right," he murmured to the other.

Sims realized they were dressed in the uniform of the US Coast Guard. Relief washed over him.

"Thank God," he said. "I knew you'd find us."

The coast guard officers looked at him blankly.

"Watch out for that man." Sims stood up on the mattress and pointed at Fablio. "He's crazy. He attacked me. He tried to kill me."

Fablio smiled sadly and shook his head.

"Do you see what I mean, gentlemen? Isn't it the way I told you?"

One of the coast guard officers dropped the ice pick into a plastic bag. The other took Sims gently but firmly by the elbow and led him off the bed.

"You'll have to come with us, Mr. Sims."

"Yeah, sure," Sims said, looking at him strangely. "I want to go with you. I need to get to Jamaica right away. My wife and daughter are expecting me."

"I'm afraid you'll have to come back to Florida with us first to answer some questions."

"Anything you say." Sims craned his neck to look back at Fablio. "Didn't you hear what I told you? That man's a maniac. He tried to kill me."

"Sure, sure. Mind your step."

He escorted Sims up a flight of steps and onto the deck, never once releasing his grip. The coast guard cutter lay near alongside rocking gently on the waves.

"It was the damnedest thing you ever saw," Sims said. "They pulled me off the wreck of my sailboat, and there were people everywhere having a cocktail party. Then suddenly they were all gone, and this maniac was in my bed. I thought he was a woman. He tried to kill me so I had to tie him up. You can see that, can't you? It was self-defense, plain and simple."

Sims realized that he was babbling and abruptly closed his mouth. A cold hand of apprehension settled around his heart and began to squeeze. Suddenly he saw how the situation might be misinterpreted, how easy it would be to mislead an innocent observer. A clever liar could twist the facts. What had Fablio said while they were untying him, while Sims lolled unconscious with the ice pick across his lap?

They drew nearer to the rail. Another smaller boat floated beside the cutter. Sims realized it was the missing lifeboat from the yacht. He was not surprised. The night had been calm. Cast adrift on the same current, the lifeboat would not have wandered far.

The lifeboat was loosely draped with a black plastic tarp that ruffled in the awakening morning breeze. At first Sims thought it was heaped full of fish. Something bulged unequally beneath the plastic. Then the stiffening breeze peeled the tarp half off. One of the crew of the cutter who was in the bow of the lifeboat caught the black sheet and pulled it back across the boat, fastening it down with a line, but not before Sims saw what the boat contained.

He turned slowly and found the two coast guard officers looking at him, and standing behind them Fablio, his bloody, damaged European features a study of polite concern. The whole world seemed to revolve under his feet. He caught at the rail before he fell, and vomited.

"Poor Mr. Sims," he heard the Italian say as darkness closed over his sight. "You see, gentlemen, this whole business has been too much for him."

THE NAIL

"We have rats," said John Martin in a conversational tone.

"Really?" Melissa coated a slice of toast with golden marmalade and bit into it. "How do you know?"

Her husband sipped steaming coffee so as not to burn his lips.

"I heard them last night while you were asleep."

Fastidiously, she dabbed a gleaming marmalade pearl from the page of her book.

"What do they sound like?"

"Scratching. Banging. Tapping. They make a lot of noise. You'd think they were three feet long."

She shuddered.

"We'll have to buy poison."

"Traps, I think."

"No, poison is best – it kills them all. At least, that's what my father always said."

"We'll see."

They had rented the old farmhouse on the South Shore of Nova Scotia for the summer. The house was furnished and boasted electric lights and indoor plumbing. The long month of August stretched before them, an unbroken prospect of solitude and leisure.

"Maybe it's not rats at all," he said, mischievous sparks in his blue eyes. "Maybe it's the ghost of Miss Small."

Miss Small, an elderly spinster, had been the last permanent resident in the house. After her ailing father died she chose to live on alone. One summer when her relatives had not heard from her for several weeks they came out to the house to investigate. They found the door unlocked, food moldering on the kitchen table, the clothes in her closet undisturbed, but no trace of the old woman.

"The odd thing about it," said the real estate agent with gusto, for he held the signed rental papers in his hand, "was that it was so out of character. Miss Small was a practical, resourceful woman. Not the kind to run off. She did her own gardening and maintenance, and was said to be in perfect health."

"And she was never heard from again?" asked John Martin.

"Not a word. After seven years her nephew decided to sell the house, but had trouble finding a buyer because of its remote location, so he began renting it out."

"Have many others stayed in the house before us?" Melissa asked nervously.

"Oh, yes. It's very popular in the summertime. You have your own private sand beach. I'm told you can live here for days and not see another soul."

That night as they lay in bed upstairs, Melissa had trouble sleeping. An image of rats scurrying through the walls formed itself on the darkness whenever her mind began to drift, their greasy brown fur bristling and their naked, pink tails slimy with filth, their eyes bright little tacks.

Beside her the breaths of her husband deepened. The leaves of trees rustled in the gentle sea breeze outside the open bedroom window. All else was stillness.

Dreamily she began to lose the thread of her thoughts. A sense of unreality stole over her. She forgot whether her eyes were open or shut. The noises crept in upon her awareness with imperceptible guile so that at some point she became conscious of them, but had no recollection of their beginning. She listened to them without alarm, as though they were voices in a dream.

A regular tap-tap-tap followed by silence, then a rustling clatter and a groan of wood, again with a period of silence. This sequence repeated itself with rhythmic insistence. It seemed to come from some indefinable part of the house. She tried to trace the sounds in her mind but their origin eluded her.

There was an unnatural quality to the tapping. It was not a random animal sound but measured and deliberate, almost a signal. When she began to focus her awareness the noises dimmed and stopped, but when she allowed her weary thoughts to drift toward sleep they started again, as though whatever made the sounds could sense her alertness.

"I heard your rats last night," she said, lying in bed watching her husband dress.

"Noisy little vermin, aren't they?"

"John, you have to get rid of them – I can't stand that every night."

He pulled a short-sleeved shirt over his head and tucked it into his cotton trousers.

"Anyway, I think I know where they're hiding." His tone was mysterious.

"What do you mean?"

"I did some exploring this morning while you were asleep. Get dressed and I'll show you."

She put on jeans and a blouse and followed him into the upstairs hall. He led her to the far end where the roof sloped down. It was cluttered with unused furniture and cardboard boxes filled with old magazines, broken ornaments and other bric-a-brac. Silently he began to clear the wall.

"What are you doing?" she asked.

"There's a windowless gable on the other side of this wall. It must have a door somewhere – here it is."

He peeled back a corner of faded wallpaper to reveal the edge of a tiny door no more than two feet high. It had been papered over, and in the dimness that lay at the end of the hall the crack in the wallpaper that defined the door was almost invisible.

"Aren't you clever," she said with delight.

He preened himself.

"Simple deduction."

Carefully, he slid his hand down the edge of the door under the loose wallpaper. There was a metallic clank. He pulled the door open with difficulty, its iron hinges groaning with rust. It was the full thickness of the wall and formed on both sides of the same rough-sawn hardwood planks that made up the frame of the house. A musty odor exhaled from the darkness.

"John, look!" she said, grasping her husband by the elbow as he crouched beside her. She pointed at the inner surface of the door.

The age-darkened wood had been worried away splinter by splinter into a depression an inch deep the size of her hand. There were scratches and chips all over the door, but most were concentrated on the edge behind the latch. The floor of the shadowy chamber beyond was littered with tiny bits of wood.

"They're game little bastards," he said with sour humor. "It would take more than a year to chew through this door."

He fell to his hands and began to crawl forward.

"Where are you going?" she asked in alarm.

"To take a look around."

"What if they're in there? You might get bitten."

"There's no danger unless you corner them," he said firmly.

For several seconds she heard him rustling about. Then there was silence.

"Did you find anything?" she called nervously.

His head thrust out and made her jump. He stared at her, cheeks ashen and mouth agape, a look of shock on his face. She screamed softly and covered her mouth. The sight of her fear seemed to snap him back to himself.

"There's a body," he said, swallowing dryly. "A dead body. I think it must be Miss Small."

Without another word he disappeared back into the darkness. She crouched wide-eyed before the black square of the open door.

"John, if this is a joke I'll never speak to you again," she said tremulously.

"Come and see for yourself." His voice drifted from somewhere farther beyond. "There's no danger – she's been dead for ages."

She inched to the door and peered within but could see only blackness.

"You're blocking the light," he said in annoyance. "Either come in or back away."

Sliding to one side, she sat on her heels and stared at the inner surface of the door where the wood had been eroded away. It was covered with hundreds of small round holes that appeared to have been caused by some kind of insect or worm. After a few minutes she crawled to the opening and put her head inside.

"I'm coming in," she said loudly.

There was no answer.

Cautiously she entered the darkness and sat letting her eyes adjust to the pallid glow that slid through from the hall.

"You can stand up," said her husband, his voice startlingly near.

He helped her to her feet and drew her farther in. Something brushed her face. She gasped and reached up, then realized it was only a cobweb.

Etched in the dim light from the doorway, the shriveled body of a woman lay in a grotesque sprawling posture on the floor. Her dried eye sockets stared blindly upwards and her blackened lips shrank away from her teeth in a death grin.

"She's mummified," he said with a mixture of revulsion and interest.

"What could have happened?" she whispered.

He bent and picked up something from beside the outstretched hand of the corpse, then held it to the light. It was a hammer, its wooden shaft covered with dust, its head rusty.

"She must have come in here to fix something," he said.

"You don't suppose she was murdered?"

He bent over the corpse, studying it.

"I don't see any sign of foul play. The police may be able to find something."

"She locked herself in," Melissa said with sudden insight. "She used the hammer to try to break out, but couldn't."

Going to the door and pulling it half-shut with a groan of protest from the hinges, her husband examined the depression.

"I think you're right," he murmured, matching the head of the hammer to several dents. "These holes are nail holes. She must have used a nail to try to chisel out the lock on the door, but the door was too thick and the wood too hard. Imagine it. She must have sat for days in pitch darkness tapping away with this hammer on a nail by touch alone, not able to see what she was doing. What incredible determination."

A chill went through Melissa. She remembered the tap-tap-tapping in her dream.

"John, let's get out of here now, please."

"In a minute," he said absently.

He moved back and forth across the hidden chamber, back bent and eyes directed at the dusty floor.

"John, did you hear me? What are you doing?"

"Looking for the nail. It has to be here somewhere."

"It doesn't matter. Let's just go," she insisted. A sense of indefinable dread spread itself across her heart and muffled its beats.

Against her will, her eyes were drawn to the grinning face of the corpse. To her heated imagination it seemed to wear an expression of possessive glee. She traced with reluctance the frozen lines in its cheeks and between its gathered brows, letting her eyes range upward until they stopped upon a small, round button in the center of its forehead that was half hidden by a wisp of gray hair.

The features of the corpse dimmed. For a moment she thought she was fainting. Then she realized the small door had begun to swing shut. Her husband, quicker than she, almost reached it before the sharp metallic clink of its iron lock signaled the futility of his effort.

He began to pound the door with the hammer he still held in his hands. She heard the thuds but could not see him. Within the room lay total darkness. She heard a clatter as he dropped the hammer onto the floor, then duller thuds made by his feet as he tried to kick the door open. It seemed to take him several minutes to grasp the reality of their situation, which she had apprehended with a flash of intuition from the first.

"Oh, God," he said in a soft voice, repeating the words over and over in a kind of primal prayer.

Numb, she got on her hands and knees and crawled to the corpse. Her mind was detached. She felt along the outline of its dried limbs, reaching toward its face. Somewhere inside her the horror screamed, but she paid no attention. Her husband heard the dry rustle of her fingers on the leathery cover of the dead woman's skull.

"Melissa, what are you doing?"

"We'll need the nail," she said.

THE GLEN OF THE GREEN WOMEN

O hone a rie'! O hone a rie'!
  The pride of Albin's line is o'er,
And fall'n Glenartney's stateliest tree;
We ne're shall see Lord Ronald more!
                    – from Scott's "Glenfinlas"

It was the fall of the year, just at that time when the frost first begins to sparkle on brown leaves in the moonlight. Lord Ronald and Lord Douglas had become separated from their hunting party the day before during the heat of the chase, and now they rode along through the gathering dusk joking and laughing after the manner of young men freed from the constraint of polite society.

Their spirits were high, for it happened that their trail had been the true one. All the afternoon before and from the first light of morning they had followed the blood spoor of the wounded stag, finally running it to ground and giving it peace with twin arrows in its heart. The antlered carcass swung heavily at Lord Ronald's saddlebow, and both youths were finding much pleasure in anticipating the discontent of the party when they showed their prize.

They were new companions, having met only ten days before when the hunt was formed. Flowing locks black as the raven's wing framed the dark face of Lord Ronald, while his companion was blonde and golden with eyes blue as heaven. Their friendship had flowered quickly. Equal rank removed the necessity for reserve, and their natures were similar, save that Lord Douglas had a strain of thoughtfulness he could not always laugh away.

He took care to see that it did not hinder his fun, and to keep his spirits light he would often sing gay ballads and madrigals as they rode, his clear Highland voice echoing in his friend's laughter while the notes of his lute hung on the crisp air. Neither could have found a more amiable companion, and their happiness would have been complete except for the absence of the fairer sex, which lack they often had occasion to bemoan.

The last shaft of the dying sun winked out behind the western hills and left them in the forest gloom with tall black pines rearing silent all around, their needled branches touching above the riders' heads. Everything was stillness. The hooves of the horses fell mute on the soft forest floor, and both men ceased to speak with the waning of the sun, oppressed by the sense of timeless mouldering decay that emanated from the green shadows. The very air seemed listening, as though attentive ears had frozen windless behind each tree to mark their passage.

As they penetrated ever deeper toward the heart of the wood, the mood of menace grew upon them. Lord Douglas unthinking began to still the rhythmic creak of his saddle leather with the palm of his hand, though there was scant need – in the dead air the sound was as dull as if encased in cotton. In his heart was the urge to go quickly and unseen. Lord Ronald's brow was knitted and his proud mouth grimly set, but he gave no other sign.

They heard the dull drip-splash of slow water and followed it to a black stream flowing westward in the hollow of the valley. The stream moved thickly around moss-covered rocks and through the brown fingers of drooping willow branches, a lethargic meanderer between mossy toadstooled banks. Dead vegetation revolved and tangled like wisps of hair on its surface. If any creature lived in its depths, it was not to be seen.

Onward they rode with the stream on their left hand. They had all but lost the light of day, and the brightest stars were glowing through the gaps above their heads, when they came upon a small grassy clearing where they discovered to their pleasure a rude bothy, built and abandoned by some previous hunting expedition that had passed through the glen.

The prospect of shelter for the night at once revived Lord Ronald's spirits. With a shout that fled unheeded through the heavy boughs, he spurred his horse toward the hut.

Lord Douglas followed more slowly, smiling a bleak smile at his friend's display. He too was much cheered at the thought of spending the night within four walls, no matter how rough those might be. The evil humor that had settled upon him began to dissolve away until once again the wood seemed no more threatening than a country garden.

They secured their mounts and suspended the stag from the branch of a nearby tree to keep it safe from wild animals – but before so doing they took care to cut their evening meal from off its tender hind quarters. The bothy boasted a primitive hearth in the center of the floor, with a hole in the roof to let the smoke out. By full darkness they were secure inside, feasting on roast venison and whiskey, and reliving the excitement of the hunt, the stag's crimson breath and the nobility of its defiant stand.

Eventually, after every detail had been told and told again, their thoughts turned inward to the grassy hills and shaded lanes of their homes. Past follies were called up for the other's approval amid the growing camaraderie produced by the strong drink. Each felt the other's friends to be his own. Lord Ronald opened another bottle while Lord Douglas got out his lute and began to sing lusty hunting songs of long ago. The full moon rose high and sent her silver light through the smoke hole into the bothy, and the fire burned dull red.

"Truly, Douglas," Lord Ronald spoke when his friend had done, "this would be a brave party if only we had two lasses for company."

Lord Douglas was in the act of smiling agreement when suddenly from near without there came a merry singing in high sylvan voices. Fear quickened in them, for at first they suspected a robber's trick to murder them and steal their horses and possessions. Though both were clumsy with drink, Lord Ronald drew his sword and cast dry wood on the fire, and Lord Douglas notched an arrow to his hunting bow. The sound grew louder – then without warning the door burst open and two lithe maidens entered singing and dancing.

They laughed to see the tense stance of the lords and chidingly asked them if they must defend themselves against unarmed girls, all the while continuing to move graceful limbs in the flickering light of the fire. Lord

Ronald and Lord Douglas were amazed that such comely maidens should be abroad in the forest at night. Sheepishly they lowered naked points and stood swaying, watching the sinuous dance with wonder and growing delight. Alike the girls had golden hair and flowing gowns of forest green that moved with their bodies as the seaweed with the waves. They seemed to be sisters, if not twins: the eyes of both were lit by the same glow, burning languidly beneath half-lowered lashes.

They said little, but their courtly speech bespoke a higher birth than peasant stock. When Lord Ronald asked what pressing need had led them out into the darkness, they smiled a secret smile to one another.

"We came to keep you company," they said, and would not say more.

"Were you not afraid to venture near a strange camp so far from your father's house?" asked Lord Douglas.

"Nay, lord," one replied. "We saw your stag and knew you for fine gentlemen, for who else would dare kill so great a beast?"

Lord Ronald laughed and drew her close, but Lord Douglas was still uneasy in his mind. With a word to his unheeding friend he left the bothy, drawn sword in hand, and made a circle around the open green, standing to listen beside the brooding black willows at its edge. There was no sign of men, only stripes of inky darkness and the silver of the moon. The shadowed stag still hung secure on its tether.

Somewhat relieved, he went back into the shelter, but his thoughts remained troubled; and when the other maiden came near and sat beside him, he offered her little encouragement, smiling only when she smiled, and then weakly, more by way of politeness than mirth. He wondered at the timeliness of their arrival so quick on the heels of his friend's vain wish, and thought it more than natural, for in all the day's riding they had not seen a single soul.

None the less as the night wore on he forgot his unease. His three companions seemed intent on making a gay time of it. The women would not eat of the venison, but they wet their lips with the whiskey, and soon the laughter and talk became very free. Modest maidens would have blushed to hear such raillery, but no tint graced their fair cheeks. Instead their eyes sparkled in the fire glow and their teeth shone white behind full red lips. Merely to look upon them was to raise amour in the hearts of the young men. Lord Douglas touched his box and sang soft ballads of love while his friend bent and whispered words into his lady's attentive ear.

The flames on the hearth fell silent and the embers cooled from yellow to orange, and then to sooty-red. When sleep had begun to blur his fingers on the lute strings, Lord Douglas was roused by the sound of Lord Ronald stumbling to his feet, supported on the arms of the merry maiden at his side.

"Don't stir yourself, Douglas," he said pleasantly. "I've only decided to show this lass the moonlight."

They went out of the bothy, pulling the door shut behind them, and their laughter and footfalls could be heard for a little while fading into the distance.

Lord Douglas's dulled senses became aware of the other girl, sitting beyond the reach of the hearth fire with her legs drawn under her, watching him. In the stillness her quick breathing sounded unnaturally harsh to his ears. Wishing to recapture the careless spirit he had known before, he began to play and sing once again – but the music had no power to lift his heart, and when he paused, he heard her breaths more loudly than before. His eyes sought her in the gloom. Now she seemed to be leaning forward on her hands toward him, her hair falling and shrouding her face, hiding it in blackest shadow.

For no reason he could ken Lord Douglas shivered and became afraid. The music went from his head and his stilled hands dropped from the strings. In his fancy the girl's somber shadow seemed to grow and take on the feline grace of a great cat knotted to spring. The air hissed softly between her teeth. When she moved her head, catlike her eyes caught the ember-glow and shone redly in her darkened face with the color of hellfire.

A dread that he had fallen into the toils of some fell power began to form itself in Lord Douglas's soul. The bestial crouch of the creature, who thought herself invisible in the darkness, her sudden wordless watchfulness as she waited for him to fall asleep – these things raised the hackles on his neck, yet he dared not challenge her with speech lest she immediately spring upon him and seek his throat. Vividly he recalled the long forgotten tales of his old nurse concerning were-creatures: human-like demons who by the light of the moon sprout rending fangs and claws and go out in search of human flesh.

He despaired of reaching his sword before the she-thing might be upon him, and doubted the effectiveness of the steel in any case; yet he knew he must not delay lest she imagine him deep asleep and so an easy kill. In his desperation he recalled hearing it said that the creatures of hell were much discomforted by holy music, and grasping at this straw he began to play and sing with a chill heart an ancient lay he had learned as a child in praise of the blessed Virgin.

Gnashing frustration, the shadow drew back to its original place.

"I thought you asleep, my lord," the maiden's mellow voice crooned sweetly.

"On such a night as this I feel more need of song than sleep," spoke Lord Douglas, alive to the game although the sweat stood cold on his brow; nor once did he cease the melody he had begun.

"My lord, end your song, for it is painful to my ears." Her pleading voice was gentle, promising much gratitude.

"Nay, I will not. This is a holy lay, and I have the wish to hear it."

So he played on through the long night. When he would finish the song, immediately he would begin it again, singing the words over and over until they became a chanted prayer. Many times she begged him to stop, but he closed his ears to her enticements.

The fire burned out and left him in blind darkness, for he dared not pause to add wood to the coals. Oftentimes above the music of his lute he heard the sound of a heavy body shifting, and the click of claws against stones in the earthen floor. She would come near to him and breathe her fetid breath against his cheek until his hands trembled, yet still he played on with leaden fingers, and sang with a throat that burned like fire.

The whisky he had drunk and the droning words of the song mingled in his brain and made his eyelids droop, though he fought with all his will against sleep. Dawn was an eternity away. And all the while her honeyed voice lulled him, promising to cradle his head on her knee, to sooth his brow with her kisses and her cool fingertips as he dreamed of summer.

Mad hallucinations danced before his sight. Many times he forgot why he must play, and paused until the novelty of silence woke him with a start to his peril. At last, after an eternity of valiant struggle, as the first light of dawn seen through the smoke hole overhead was casting its gossamer veil across the stars, the lute slipped from his unconscious hands and clattered to the ground.

Dimly, as from a vast distance, he sensed a black shape loom over him. The blackness grew and spread until he was certain he must be enveloped by it. Then suddenly with a rush of wings and a mournful cry, it dissolved into mist and vanished. From that dim other place he heard the enraged scream of a beast, followed by a crash like thunder that receded into silence – things which were as nothing to him, for he was beyond care. And last before he entered a dreamless sleep, although he could not be certain of it, he felt a gentle kiss upon his brow and smelled the scent of jasmine.

On the morrow when he awoke, Lord Douglas found great claw marks in the earthen floor and on the walls of the bothy. The stout door had been shattered outward by a hurtling force and lay scattered for some distance around on the grass. Ground beneath a heavy foot, his lute had been bitten into pieces. He ventured cautiously out and discovered both stag and horses gone. Where the great prize had hung remained only a mocking shred of leather thong that moved gently to-and-fro in the light breeze. Lord Ronald was nowhere to be seen.

Lord Douglas began to call for his friend with a heavy voice, for in his heart there was no hope. At the same time he gave silent thanks to the Blessed Virgin for sparing his own life, for he knew only a divine power could have prevailed against the iron-thewed strength of that fiendish succubus, the evidence of which was all about him. He feared to go from the clearing into the wood lest the demon should still be waiting there to fall upon him; but when his loudest shouts brought no response, he thought of Lord Ronald perhaps lying hurt or dying among the browning ferns on the forest floor, and put aside his self-concern. Finding his sword where the monster had cast it, he took it up and began to range carefully through the undergrowth.

After some minutes of futile search he came upon a sheltered hollow not an arrow's flight north of the bothy's door. Pressing through the dense shrubs that lined its edge, suddenly he became as stone. His heart quickened in horror and his tongue clove mute at the sight that greeted him.

There upon the rank grass lay a heap of human bones, red with blood but sucked clean of flesh. They had been scattered about by a careless hand. Some had been cracked open for the inner marrow. A short distance away was the bloody skull, stripped of its cover, and Lord Douglas cringed to look upon it, for in cruel jest the antlers of the stag had been thrust deep into its gaping eye sockets. It rested upright in the grass with the great red-stained antlers spreading out like the naked limbs of a tree from its blindness.

Men say that Lord Douglas was changed from that day forward. A Bible was ever in his hand, and he kept the Sabbath with a zeal most considered unhealthy in so young a man. Nor would he speak of what he had seen in the dark wood, but maintained a solemn counsel behind wild eyes.

JANUS

Through the sour, sweat-stick air in the dimly lit carnival tent, the drifter first saw her face. It was the face of a goddess and a child, both old and young, a silver shadow from adolescent dreams long ceased to come in the night but recalled vividly in an instant by its shining purity. Skin ivory cool, eyes dark pools of meaning, lips curved in a subtle yet enigmatic smile ripe with promise. It was the face of a fallen angel of terrible beauty.

She looked down at him from the dirty wooden stage over the heads of the gap-mouthed local crowd. Time held its breath as the silence spoke to him. Waves of vertigo rose from some inner sea. He would have stumbled but for the dank press of sweat-stained bodies around him.

Eagerly, he traced the line of her brow, the regal straightness of her nose, the graceful curve of her cheek, his eyes restless, then frantic, as he tried vainly to memorize her perfection before it vanished and he awoke in his rented flophouse room with its fly-specked wallpaper and the drip-drip of rusty water in the sink.

But this was no dream. He became aware of the muttering voices in the crowd as though returning from a far place.

"Shit, it's a goddamn fake."

"Can't be – look at them eyes."

"Well I never …"

"How'd you like to kiss that, Buck? Mooch-mooch!"

"Kiss my ass, Charlie."

A bulk of a man in dungarees supported by red suspenders and a cheque shirt with the sleeves rolled climbed ponderously onto the stage and stood

33

in front of the spotlight. Catcalls and hisses greeted him. He clamped a fat cigar in the corner of his mouth and raised his glistening palms. The cigar smell drifted through the heat of the thick tent air.

"That's it, folks. Last show's over. Y'all come again next year. Go out that there door on your left."

He stepped back and reached to rake a soiled gray curtain on steel rings along a pipe to hide the small stage.

Naked electric bulbs flickered to life inside the tent. Blinking screwed-up eyes and spitting tobacco juice on the sawdust, young men in checked shirts with the sleeves rolled up shuffled into the night, their giggling girlfriends clinging to their arms

Crushed boxes of popcorn and flattened candy wrappers emerged from the retreating tide of feet. In the sudden quiet, the distant music of the carousel danced ghost-like across the beaten grass.

The big man ducked around the edge of the curtain. He stopped when he saw the drifter and frowned. Rolls of skin thick as fingers gathered between his hairy eyebrows.

"What do you want, bud? Show's over."

The drifter looked from side to side and for the first time realized he stood alone before the stage. Feebly, he grinned. One of his front teeth was chipped.

"I never knowed –" He paused and took a breath. "That right, what you said? About this show being the last? I never been before tonight."

While he spoke he tried to peer past the heavy body through the crack at the edge of the curtain. He saw movement in the shadows and inwardly cursed the fat carnie.

"This is it," grunted the big man. "We'll be through town again next year. Maybe. Times is tough."

The drifter nodded agreeably, felt sweat trickle over his upper lip and wiped it off.

"I never knowed, or I'd have come last night. Hell, I'd have come every night last week." He inclined his head at the curtain. "I'd sure like another look."

"The hell you would. This here's a depression, bud. I ain't no WPA."

"I got money. I worked today – listen."

He shoved his hand deep into his pocket and the jingle of coins mingled with the music of the carousel.

The carnie narrow-eyed him with contempt.

"You don't look like you're worth spit on a hot brick. When the last show's over my man likes to relax. That's our arrangement."

"You could ask him. I got every part of a whole dollar in my pocket."

The carnie took his well-chewed cigar stub between his sausage fingers and regarded its smoldering end, hooding his thoughts beneath heavy lids.

"What the hell, it's the last night and all. He might not mind so much. I'll have a word." He started behind the curtain, then pointed with the cigar. "Stay put, hear?"

The steel rings shrieked along the pipe. From behind the frayed cotton panel, voices murmured, the carnie's deep and persuasive, and another voice that was high-pitched and feminine, protesting in a hissing whisper that ended in a curse in some foreign language.

The big man reappeared. He puffed smoke and spat a bit of tobacco leaf without taking the cigar from his mouth.

"He don't like the idea. You heard him. But he'll do it for me. He knows I treat him right."

With a grunt he crouched and eased his bulk off the stage.

"Let's see the dough."

The coins clinked one after another into the carnie's broad palm. He weighed them and closed his fist.

"Trailer's in back. Come on, I'll show you."

His beefy arm dropped over the shoulder of the drifter and tugged. The drifter let himself be pulled along, feeling the body heat of the big man against his side.

As they rounded the stage he saw that it was now bare behind the curtain. A slit door in the back wall of the tent hung open to the night. Attracted by the lights, a small white moth fluttered through. The big man threaded his hip past the flap and held it wide for the drifter to follow.

Behind the tent was black stillness. He tensed, then relaxed. Why roll him when he had no money? His mind filled with the still-fresh memory of the face, and a river of desire washed away his doubts like grains of sand and left him with short breath and a thudding heart.

They stopped at a wooden trailer. Thick lips grinning in the dark, the carnie yanked open the door. Yellow light poured like oil through the frame.

"Go on up – he's waiting. Make sure you get your money's worth, chump."

The drifter climbed the steps and felt the trailer rock on its leaf springs. The stench of cheap liquor and sour sweat slapped his face as he passed the threshold. He tightened his jaw and swallowed down his bile.

Inside was cramped. An old sofa filled the front. In the middle of the floor, a card table supported a bottle of gin three-quarters gone with a cloudy glass inverted over its top. Beside the table was a folding chair. In the back, a shelf of books, a Victrola, an ice box thick with fingerprints, and a portable toilet with a cover.

A man in his mid-twenties sat on the edge of the sofa, leaning forward with his hands folded between his knees and his head hanging level with his shoulders. He looked up wearily at the rusty creak of the springs. His dark eyes took nothing, gave nothing. Under his matted black hair and three-day stubble of beard, he might have been handsome once, in a Latino sort of way. Might have been. Now, his cheeks sank into the bones of his face and his eyes were rimmed with purple bruises.

"So, you come to look?" he said in a voice that surprised the drifter with its mellow tenor. Below the Cuban accent lurked a note of cynicism.

The drifter nodded, swallowing again but this time not because of the stench.

The Latin pointed at the chair.

"Sit and we talk. I feel like talk tonight."

The slur in the voice could not have been the work of a few minutes. The Cuban had been drinking heavily all day.

His soil-stained hands shaking with eagerness, the drifter pulled the folding chair away from the table and sat watching the other.

"You want a drink? Sure you do. You take the glass, I don't need it."

The Cuban slopped gin into the glass, then tilted the bottle to his lips, glancing from the corner of his eye.

So you come to look?" he repeated. "Well, why not. You pay, like everybody else. In fact, you pay way too much. You buy yourself a long look, mister."

The drifter said nothing. He tightened his fingers around the glass.

Deliberately the Cuban banged the bottle down on the table and shifted around on the sofa. Hoisting his thigh over the seat, he turned his back.

"Take a good look, mister – as long as you like."

From the halo of pink flesh formed by the shaved back of the Cuban's head, she gazed out at him. Her moist red lips parted. Between them, he saw the upper row of her teeth, like matched pearls. How impossibly white her skin was, like new-fallen snow with the flush of warm blood beneath it. Her large eyes rolled to the side, then returned to stare at him. The long lashes on her eyelids trembled like the wings of an insect.

Nearness revealed details he had not noticed across the tent floor. Her eyes were not truly aware. They held an emptiness that became at times almost malignant, but there was no light of intelligence to guide them. They rolled aimlessly in their sockets as though searching for something unseen.

Her lips smiled, than rippled apart in a sudden reflexive grimace that shattered her perfect beauty. But like an image in the surface of a pool when its water is disturbed, her loveliness reformed itself and in a moment was as timeless as before.

"She's my sister, you know that?" The voice of the Cuban reflected from the trailer wall. "Her name is Céleste. That's right, she even got a name. My mother named her before we was born." He gave a short bitter laugh. "My mother, she tried to drown us in a well, but my father stopped her. They had to lock her up in the asylum. She went loco, you know? Too bad."

The drifter cleared his throat. "Can she say anything?"

The Cuban turned to look over his shoulder with an amused expression.

The drifter fought down the impulse to push his dark, sweating face back to the wall.

"Talk? Sure, she talk all the time. And I mean, all … the … time," he repeated with emphasis.

He seemed to sense the drifter's tension. Taking up the gin bottle, he returned his face to the wall.

Again the angel shed her light.

"Funny thing, mister – she only talk to me. Too bad. We could make a lot of money if she talk on stage."

"What does she sound like?"

The Cuban shrugged his feminine shoulders and considered.

"She – kind of whisper, you know? Real quiet, when I try to fall asleep. Sometime she whisper the whole damn night." A shiver ran down his back and he laughed to hide it. "Hell, some night I can't shut her up no matter what."

The face of Céleste inclined as he drank from the bottle, nodding smiling silent agreement.

"What does she say?" the drifter whispered, some pressure inside forcing him to speak, to extend the time in the trailer. His gaze never wavered from her dark, beguiling eyes.

"She curses. All the time, day and night. I used to try to be good to her, you know? But her filthy words never stop. I tell you something I never told nobody – my sister got the soul of a whore. If she wasn't part of me ..."

The rolling eyes in the face seemed to respond, and the dainty upper lip curled.

"Can't no doctor cut you free?"

The face shook slow negative.

"They say it would kill us. I tell them, I don't give a damn, just do it, but the bastards won't operate."

The Latin reached up and wiped sweat from his throat.

"Hot in here tonight. You mind if I take off my shirt?"

Not waiting for an answer, he pulled his sodden white undershirt over his head and dropped it damply to the floor. His golden shoulders and back glistened in the lamplight.

"I'm tired. It's been a long day."

Sighing, he drew the bottle in against his chest and lay down sideways, resting his right ear on the padded arm of the sofa. The face of Céleste looked coyly up from its inclined position, a gleam of spittle at the corner of its mouth.

"It don't matter," the Cuban mumbled. "I'll be dead soon anyhow. My stomach's shot to hell – can't even hold a drink down anymore. Hell of a life, ain't it, mister? You take a good long look. Don't cheat yourself. Good and long ..." His voice trailed off.

In minutes, he was asleep and breathing heavily with a wheezing rasp at his throat.

The drifter continued to watch the face move and stare as random nerve impulses sent ripples of expression across it. The working lips seemed to whisper strange and shocking secrets, but when he held his breath and leaned forward in the chair he could hear nothing.

Trying not to creak the floor boards, he got up and lifted the card table out of his way, then knelt beside the sofa. The face was near enough to kiss, and below it the gleaming curve of the Cuban's back. He shifted on his knees so that his shoulder no longer blocked the light from the lamp and leaned close.

The fathomless eyes flickered only inches from his own. He sensed meaning in them, some private message beyond the power of words to convey. If only he could grasp it. This was what he had been seeking unknowingly all the years of his life. If only –

His breath stirred the tiny, silken hairs on her upper lip. Her eyes blinked liquidly as though with pent up tears. Tenderly he raised his index finger to wipe the drop of saliva from the corner of her mouth. Her lips were soft and moist beneath his touch. He traced their outline, stroking the fullness of the lower lip. They parted and closed around his finger, sucking rhythmically like a newborn infant while the expressionless eyes watched him.

A wave of lust flushed hot through his loins. Not pausing to think, he gently withdrawing his finger, unbuttoned the fly of his trousers and jerked his soiled undershorts away from his leg. With trembling hands he loosened the belt of the Cuban and rolled him onto his stomach. The Cuban moaned when the drifter drew down his pants, but did not open his eyes.

The drifter poised himself over the golden body, panting short breaths like a dog in heat. She watched with languishing eyes. He jerked his loins once, and her eyes opened wide. He jerked again. Her lips parted.

"Wha' the fuck you doin'? Get off'a me, you son'a'bitch."

The Cuban's muscular buttocks rippled. He pushed himself up on his hands and began to turn his head. In despair, the drifter closed his callused hands around the drunken man's neck, digging his dirty fingernails into the soft golden throat to stifle his cries. Céleste smiled and nodded, smiled and nodded.

As the Cuban went rigid beneath him, the drifter shuddered and groaned out his own little death. He collapsed forward, his face inches from the smiling face of his lover. A drop of his sweat fell from his nose into her mouth. Through soulless eyes he gazed at her for a lingering moment, then kissed her.

Never in his sordid life, not even in his tormented dreams, had he imagined a kiss could taste so ripe. Her lips were like the sun-warmed flesh of a newly-cut peach. He traced her pearly teeth with the tip of his tongue.

Crying out, he jerked his head away. He wiped his mouth and stared without comprehension at the back of his hand. His blood, almost black in the shadow cast by his body, welled from his lower lip and dripped onto the perfect shoulder of the dead Cuban.

She laughed silently, teeth barred under lips that writhed away from pink gums, his blood staining them a deep red, her dark eyes glittering with vindictive madness. The trailer was quiet, yet somehow in his mind he heard her laughter cascade like falling shards of glass.

"What the hell you up to?" barked a harsh voice.

He turned. The hulking shoulders of the carnie blocked the lower half of the open trailer door.

"You damn pervert, you sure as hell didn't pay enough for that," the carnie growled as he took in the scene with a glance. "Hey Rube! We got a pervert here!"

The drifter lunged out a leg and caught the carnie in the temple with the heel of his boot. The big man went down as though poleaxed. From the surrounding darkness sharp voices began to call out.

He dove through the doorway over the prone body and scrambled to his feet in the dust, then ran blindly down the shadow alleys between the tents, heedless of where his feet led him, again and again seeing in the dark her exquisitely sculptured lips move to form the single word they had shaped as he leapt into the night.

TONGUE OF THE BELL

Howard Andrews knew he would murder his wife. The outcome was never in doubt, not since the night of their knock-down fight when Eleanor had vowed to sell the church and move back to New York and Daddy. She had not followed through on her threat, but it was only a matter of time before she abandoned him. Cutter O'Keith would welcome his daughter home with open arms. The old man despised Howard. That his son-in-law was a painter was proof enough to his shrewd business mind that the young man was after his money. The difference in the ages of the newlyweds merely reinforced his prejudice.

There was nothing the old man could do to stop the O'Keith estate passing to his only daughter and her husband after his death. It was entailed family money. O'Keith had not earned it himself, and he could not withhold it from his daughter in his will, even if he wished to do so. Nor were there any other living relations to come with their hands extended for their share. All these facts Howard had determined before proposing to Eleanor.

The ironic thing was that Howard genuinely loved his wife. It had meant nothing to him that she was eight years older and less than beautiful. The day she accepted his proposal had been the most satisfying day of his life. Her father's wealth, which she must inherit when the old man finally assumed his rightful station in hell, had merely made the marriage possible. He could never support a wife on his own income. In the meantime, while they waited for the evil bastard to shuffle off his mortal coil, they were able to live quite comfortably on Eleanor's allowance.

He had selected the disused church in rural Massachusetts as their new

41

home to make her happy. Her passion for redecorating amounted almost to a mania. The church had seemed ideal – a remote haven perched on a hill near a little fishing port, yet still within driving distance of Boston. His only regret was that the church had not been a surprise. Eleanor's signature had been needed on the mortgage.

Howard gazed in meditation through the window at the wrinkled gray ocean that stretched unbroken to the eastern horizon. He stood in the bell tower, forty feet above the stone and mortar foundation of the white clapboard church. The walls of the tower faced the points of the compass. One of Eleanor's first acts had been to hire workmen to replace the slatted wooden shutters in the sides of the tower with modern thermal-pane picture windows, so as to admit the greatest amount of light. She had wanted to take out the bell and turn the room into an art studio, but Howard had put his foot down, pointing out that there was ample space on the lower floor for him to paint, and that he wanted the bell to remain. In the early days of their marriage she had occasionally been willing to humor him.

He stepped back from the window and turned to study the brass bell, which glowed like beaten gold in the rays of the setting sun. It had taken a week and seven cans of Brasso to polish away the green tarnish. The silken bell cord that once had hung through the open square in the floor directly below the bell had long since rotted off its pulley, but in other respects the bell was as it must have looked a hundred years ago, when the church was performing regular services for the farmers and fishermen of the area.

Walking across the bare plank floor, he noted with pleasure the marks of broadaxes on the beams that supported the roof of the tower. He pressed his hand against the cold side of the bell. It gave slightly on its pivot. Rhythmically, he increased the swing, building it into a graceful arc. The bell was beautiful, so massive yet so finely balanced. Clear, ringing tones softly filled the tower as the clapper kissed the inner surface of the brass. Howard never dared ring the bell more forcefully, fearing that the waves of sound would blow out the glass from the new windows.

He was about to ease the bell to a stop when its mellow tones abruptly ceased. After a second, he heard a dull thud on the wooden floor of the hall below.

Kneeling, he crawled under the bell and peered down through the open trapdoor. On the floor lay the bell clapper. The corroded stem of the clapper had snapped from its pivot. He would have to hire a welder to braze it back into place, he mused. Sighing, he straightened and descended the staircase that wrapped around the four walls inside the tower. Eleanor had taken the car to do some shopping, and would return shortly. He wondered how she would react to the dent in her newly-laid hardwood floor.

It was not until he stood in the hall, staring up at the dark circle of the bell, with the clapper, a lump of cold metal as large as his fist, weighing heavily in his hand, that the method of murder came to him. He froze like a statue in the deepening gloom, running it through his mind again and again like a song. He perceived no flaw.

Crossing into the room Eleanor had adopted for her study, he slid a leaf of notepaper from the box on her desk. He had to hurry – she might return at any moment. Taking a pencil from the mug she kept them in, he scribbled words on the paper. What he wrote did not matter, only that it was bold enough to catch her eye.

The sound of a car climbing the steep slope of the driveway caused him to hasten into the hall. He laid the paper directly over the dent made by the clapper and snapped on the hall light. Swinging the clapper in his hand nervously, he mounted the stairs of the tower two at a time and stretched himself out on the floor on his stomach, with his head projecting over the open trap beneath the bell. He waited, the clapper cradled in his hands.

The thunk of the car door was followed by the rattle of a key in the lock. Eleanor was a native New Yorker and insisted that the door be kept locked at all times. Her heels clicked in the hall.

"Howard, I'm home," she called out in her strident, high voice. "Howard, where are you?"

Howard held his breath and discovered that he was sweating. He watched a silver droplet fall from the point of his nose through the hatch and strike the paper far below. With a silent curse, he raked his shirtsleeve across his face.

Again he heard the click of her heels, then the rustle of plastic as she set her shopping bags down. A coat hanger scraped on the rod in the hall closet. He worked the clapper around in his moist fingers and extended his arms over the void of the trap. His aim must be perfect. If he missed, he doubted he had the nerve to run down the stairs and bludgeon her to death. The thought made him shudder.

"Howard? Howard, answer me, for Christ sake. I hope you aren't in one of your sulks."

The click of her heels drew nearer. He saw her below, her long mane of glossy black hair gleaming in the glow of the hall light.

She bent and picked up the paper, turned it over curiously, then read what was written on it in a low murmur.

"The last, for which the first was made."

The words surprised Howard. He had no memory of what he had scribbled in haste.

Her skull crunched like the shell of an egg as the clapper broke through. She collapsed straight down, legs and arms tumbling over each other, then toppled slowly onto her shoulder. A spot of red appeared on the floor beside her distorted hair. He saw her open mouth and staring, unfocused eye.

❦

The official inquiry into his wife's death delayed her funeral, but it passed without incident. Of course the police were suspicious, but there was little they could do. Freak deaths of this kind did sometimes occur. Cutter O'Keith hired a private investigator and applied pressure to keep the case open, but in the end nothing came of it. As a countermeasure, Howard hired a law firm to insure that his father-in-law did not attempt to block his rightful inheritance, and settled down to wait. He could afford to be patient.

He found himself alone with the open coffin at the funeral parlor. Eleanor's friends had come and gone with their condolences. He looked down impassively at the face of his dead wife, noting with an artist's professional detachment that the mortician had applied too much rouge to her cheeks. He had expected to feel nothing, but to his surprise his heart almost sang for joy. For the first time since his wedding he felt free. The sum of money he had realized from the sale of several pieces of Eleanor's jewelry enabled him to do whatever he wanted until his wife's estate was finally settled.

Glancing cautiously at the open doorway, he reached into his coat pocket and drew out the bell clapper. The police had returned it after examining it. They had found his fingerprints all over it, but that was to be expected, since in his grief upon discovering his wife's body, he had imprudently removed the bloody clapper from the hole in her skull.

He was taking a risk, he knew, but he could not stand to have the thing in the church with him, and what better way to dispose of it than with the woman whose life it had taken? He reached into the coffin and pulled her corpse aside, then slid the pear-shaped lump of metal under the small of her back. Let her sleep on that for eternity, he thought, and almost laughed aloud in hysterical relief.

∂◊

Weeks passed. The New England winter descended with its iron grip and locked the coast beneath snow and ice. The scattered houses around the church, columns of white smoke rising from their frosted chimneys, resembled a picture postcard. Howard barely noticed the beauty. Although he had planned to spend the winter in the south of France, somehow he never got around to buying the plane ticket. He stayed inside the church, only going out when forced to get groceries or pick up his mail, and he began to drink heavily. The locals often saw him when they passed along the road, standing in the window of the bell tower, staring out at the sea.

Howard found himself drawn compulsively to the tower. He liked to lose himself in the view, but carefully avoided the bell with his eyes. Had he possessed the strength, he would have hurled it into the ocean waves. Its mute bulk reproached him, and in his fits of brooding he sometimes fancied that, had he not taken its tongue and deprived it of speech, it would have betrayed him. As soon as it might pass without comment, he promised himself, he would hire workmen and have the damn thing removed.

Descending the tower, he went into Eleanor's study and sat at her desk. On the desk was a soiled water tumbler and half a bottle of rye. He slopped liquor into the glass and sucked it moodily, glaring around the room. Trash lay scattered across the floor. There were broken pieces of glass from another bottle he had knocked off the desk and forgotten to clean up. The dark stain on the red carpet looked almost like dried blood.

He must have slept. He jerked erect in the chair and peered around

45

the study owlishly through bloodshot eyes, wondering what had woken him. Pale moonlight shone through the window. He picked the empty glass from his lap and set it carefully on the desk, listening. The faint click of heels sounded in the hallway, as it had sounded every night since his wife's funeral. He held his breath in expectation, his heart pounding against his ribs. A sickening crunch was followed a moment later by the dull thud of a body collapsing to the floor.

Unable to listen any longer, he struggled out of the chair and ran wildly into the hall. He had a bad moment fumbling in the dark for the light switch – then it snapped on, and he found himself looking straight upward at the motionless circle of the bell. It took an immense effort to lower his eyes to the floor. With a weak chuckle, he sagged against the oak-paneled wall, his relief so great that it sucked the strength from his legs and left him trembling. Only his nerves. Eleanor was dead, and he was free.

Something hung on the air, a sweetness that cloyed in his nostrils. It was so faint, he thought he was imagining it, until he saw wisps of smoke drifting near the ceiling. With a flash of realization, he remembered the pot of stew he had left cooking on the stove in the kitchen before climbing the tower. He had put in on for dinner, but that must have been hours ago.

He ran down the corridor toward the rear of the church. The smoke was thicker and made his eyes sting. Coughing, he opened the kitchen door. An angry blast of flames threw him backward. The entire kitchen was an inferno. Even as he watched, flames leapt through the open doorway and began to run along the ceiling of the corridor. They forced him back into the entrance hall, toward the front door. The smoke was so dense he could not see where he was going, but had to feel his way with his eyes streaming tears.

Blindly, he fumbled for the front door handle. He was not yet in a state of panic. Beyond the door lay the crisp air of a winter evening and a soft blanket of snow. He would wake up one of his neighbors and get them to phone the fire department. He rattled the latch. Fear gripped his heart for the first time when the door refused to open. He remembered locking the door earlier. The deadbolt was a double key type. Eleanor had insisted upon it as the most secure. It could only be opened from the inside with the key, and the key was sitting on the counter in the kitchen.

The flames flew like winged lizards across the walls of the hall. He saw by their glow that he was cut off from the other rooms of the renovated church. There was no escape other than the tower. Fighting to retain consciousness, he crawled on his hands and knees up the stairs into the bell chamber, and used his elbow to break out one of the windows. Smoke roiled up through the open trap in a solid column of sooty black. There was no way to close it. Under the moonlight, he could see through the broken window the houses of his nearest neighbors, their lights extinguished, their inhabitants asleep. They were too distant to hear his shouts for help. Somehow he had to wake them.

He searched wildly for something to strike against the bell. The room was empty. He had always preferred it that way. Already the flames were climbing the stairs. He laid his hands against the closed bell-chamber door and felt heat against his palms.

Staggering to the bell, he struck it as hard as he could with his clenched fist. It gave off a low tone that he could barely hear over the roar and crackle of the flames. Desperately, he began to kick and pound it, the impact of his blows rocking it gently on its pivot. The air in the room was hot, almost too hot to bear. Smoke snakes issued between the cracks in the floor and writhed around his legs. He felt his rubber-soled shoes sticking to the planks.

His streaming tears drew two soot-black tracks down his cheeks. Crying out insanely at the top of his lungs, Howard set his hands against the side of the bell. His palms hissed and crackled on the heated brass. With all the force of his back, he drove his forehead into the curved belly of the great thing. A mellow tone echoed into the night over the roar of the flames. Again he smashed his skull into the bell, and again. Nine times he struck the bell before he slid slowly down, his cheek pressed against its shimmering surface and the smeared blood from his forehead hissing on the brass. In slow motion, he tumbled thought the trap to the floor of the hall, so far below.

They found him there early the next morning. Someone noticed the east window in the bell tower broken out and called the police. Howard lay in a pool of his own blood on the floor under the trap of the tower, his skull staved in and his back broken. There was nothing to show how or why the trauma had occurred. The hall of the church was dusty but otherwise unremarkable. When the investigating policeman climbed the stairs to the bell chamber, his revolver nervously extended in his hand, he discovered only an empty room, the glass broken outward from one of its windows, and the great brass bell with its side stained red.

DREAM A LITTLE DREAM OF ME

"They say if you fall asleep in a dream, you never wake up," Kim told them with a wicked little smile on her red lips. "You think you're awake, but it's really just another dream."

"Charming," Sue said with a grimace. "Where do you get this weird stuff?"

"I don't know, some old book I read years ago."

Jason sipped his wine and looked at the faces of his friends, dancing in the red glow from the fireplace. Whose idea had it been to tell ghost stories until the power came back on? He couldn't remember. The wine made his head spin.

"You mean, you fall asleep and start to dream, and in the dream you dream you wake up?"

"That's it, Sherlock."

"But you're still asleep. You think your awake and living your normal life, but you're really still just dreaming."

Boss laughed nervously. "You guys are creeping me out."

"But what happens to your body while you are dreaming?" Jason wondered. The concept intrigued him.

"I don't know," Kim shrugged. "You lie in a coma, I guess."

"Maybe you don't exist in the real world anymore," Sue said.

"You couldn't just cease to exist. Flesh doesn't just disappear." Boss looked from Jason to Kim for confirmation.

"But if you're dreaming that you're awake, and then dream that you fall asleep, and dream that you're dreaming of being awake, maybe dreams are all that's left of you," Sue said.

The four friends pondered this in silence. One of the hardwood logs across the andirons in the fireplace cracked in the middle and sent up a shower of sparks as it collapsed onto the concrete hearth. They all flinched. Kim giggled.

"I thought we were telling ghost stories," Boss said.

"You just said you wanted to hear something scary," she reminded him. "Well, I scared you, didn't I?"

"I've heard that if you die in a dream, you die in real life." Sue said.

"I heard that one," Boss said.

Jason remained silent. He was still thinking of waking up in a dream, but not knowing it was a dream. It had happened to him more than once. It always creeped him out. When he came right down to it, how did he know he had ever wakened from the dream? Couldn't you wake up in a dream, but still be dreaming, and then go back to sleep in the dream, and wake up again, over and over? Maybe that was what happened to those who lay in a coma. Dream after nesting dream, one inside the other like Russian dolls. For that matter, how did he know he wasn't in a coma right now?

He touched the polished wood on the arm of his chair and rubbed it under the palm of his hand. It was moist with sweat. The fire in the fireplace was hotter than they needed in the small sitting room of the summer house.

"A yogi from India once told me the whole world is a dream," he murmured, staring at the fire.

"When was that?" Sue asked.

"That summer I went to Nepal on that UN student exchange program. I told you about it. The year before we met."

"I remember now. How did you meet a yogi?"

"That was a funny thing," Jason said, remembering. "I was walking along a mountain road because my motorcycle broke down. Those bikes they gave us to get around were old and they were always breaking. Anyway, I was walking along and suddenly, there he was walking beside me, a little old man with snowy white hair in a yellow robe."

"Where'd he come from?" Boss asked, grinning at Kim. "Was he a ghost?"

"Don't laugh," Jason said seriously. "I thought he was, either a ghost or some kind of spirit. But he wasn't threatening. He was a sweet old dude.

He had this weird little laugh, a kind of little titter, and he spoke English well enough that I could make out what he was saying, most of it. We got to talking as we walked along with the snow-covered mountains towering all around us and a sheer drop of about two thousand feet off the edge of the road. I had to stop to catch my breath every so often, because the air was so thin, and he waited for me while I was bent over with my hands on my knees."

"So what did he say?" Boss asked impatiently.

Jason shook his head and frowned.

"I don't remember much of it. He said something about the entire world being nothing more than a dream. Something about him dreaming me and me dreaming him. Something like that."

"Trippy," Kim said. She lifted her long-stemmed glass. "I'm dry. More wine, Bossman."

Her muscular boyfriend obediently stood up from his chair and brought an open bottle of pale golden liquid to refill her glass.

"Do you think your father will mind if we dry up his wine cellar?"

Kim smirked at him.

"Daddy is rich. He can just buy another crate."

"Where is your father, anyway?" Sue asked.

"Somewhere in Asia, I think. He flies around all over the place. I can't keep track."

"It was nice of him to let us use your summer house."

"I don't even think he knows we're here."

Lightning flashed through the drawn drapes, and a second later thunder exploded.

"We picked a great weekend," Boss said to Jason. "I hope a tree doesn't come down on your car. Maybe you should move it."

He went to the picture window and pulled the drapes back from the side to peer out. Lightning flashed again, making him draw his face back reflexively. They waited for the crash.

"Hey, I thought your car was green."

Jason looked up from the reflective surface in his wine glass.

"It is green."

"Well it's blue now."

"What? What are you talking about?"

"Take a look."

With a sigh of weariness, he set down his glass and went to the window. He couldn't see anything more than a vague outline of the car. He was about to turn away when the lightning flashed again. He stared at the after image burned into his retinas as the thunder crashed around him.

"Well?" Boss said.

"It's just a trick of the light. The lightning makes it look blue."

He returned to his chair, puzzled, trying to remember the exact shade of green on his car. It was a dark green, sort of a bluish green. Wasn't it?

"Maybe we should get into the car and drive back to the city," Sue suggested.

"We're safer here than on the mountain road," he murmured. "It's liable to be washed out in places."

"I had a funny dream once," Kim said.

"You weren't a butterfly, by any chance?" Sue asked.

"Ha, good one. No, I wasn't a butterfly."

"Why would anyone dream they were a butterfly?" Boss demanded. "That's stupid."

"Says the football jock who should know," Kim said.

"Hey! Watch your mouth, girl."

"Or what? You going to wrestle me?"

"Right after we go to bed."

"Big promise. You'll be snoring from all the wine you've had."

"You drank more than I did."

"It doesn't put me to sleep."

"Right. Little Miss Perfect."

"I am."

Jason looked across at Sue, who rolled her eyes. He stared at her thoughtfully. There was something odd about her appearance. What was it? Her hair, that was it.

Boss got up, staggered to catch his balance, and pulled Kim up from the couch by the hand. She giggled and waved at Sue, who returned the gesture, and the couple stumbled into the entrance hall, moving toward the stairs.

"When did you dye your hair blonde?" Jason asked.

Sue blinked at him in surprise.

"I don't know, months ago. Why?"

"That can't be right. It was brown yesterday."

"Sorry, marine. I haven't been a brunette for a long time."

"But that can't be right." He shook his head. The wine was making it hard to think. He remembered her at lunch the other day, and her hair had been brown. Or had it?

"You're drunk. I'm going to bed." She pushed herself up from the couch and disappeared up the stairs.

❧

He sat in the empty parlour, feeling the heat from the fireplace against his legs, listening to the rolling thunder, which had passed over the mountain and was now moving away. After a while, his head rolled to the side, and he began to snore. A sound startled him.

A little, elderly woman in a flowered dress that looked like it belonged in a Norman Rockwell painting came into the room through the door to the kitchen and sat down in the chair opposite his. From a large leather bag she took a ball of bright red yarn and two long knitting needles, and began to knit. She had on those half-lens, wire-frame reading glasses that are cut through the middle and sit on the end of your nose. Her shrivelled face was like the skin of a baked apple.

"Where did you come from?" Jason said.

"I was in the kitchen," she said without looking at him. Her voice had the scratchiness of age

"No, I mean, who are you? Why are you here?"

"I live here."

Jason stared at her. For some reason, he felt no emotion, not even surprise.

"Are you related to Kimberly Stein?"

"I'm her great aunt."

"You were here, in the house, the whole time we've been here?"

She glanced at him and smiled.

"I seldom leave the house, young man."

He digested this in confusion. He had been all over the house. How could he have missed seeing the old woman? Why didn't Kim mention that she was living here?

The only sound was the click of her knitting needles. She made a little noise of annoyance and took from her leather bag a large pair of dress-making scissors, then used them to snip off a ragged strand of yarn from whatever she was knitting.

"You should have come and sat with us," he said, not knowing what else to say.

"I don't like a lot of commotion," she said, shaking her head.

"I hope we're not putting you out, staying here over the weekend."

"Not at all. It gets lonely here sometimes."

Jason wondered if she lived here all year round, or had an apartment in the city. The summer house was pretty remote.

"I heard you telling ghost stories," the old woman said. "I know a ghost story. Would you like to hear it?"

He hesitated, then shrugged.

"Sure, why not."

What else was he going to say?

"Well, as the story goes, the woman who used to live in this house lost her mind after her husband died. It was the solitude, you see. She wasn't used to living alone, and the long winter nights started to make her hear voices and see things in the shadows."

"When was this?"

"Many years go."

"So what happened to her?"

"Her mind got worse and worse until she took a rope and looped it over that hook in the beam. See it up there?"

He looked up at the cathedral ceiling and saw that there was indeed a metal hook screwed into the angled beam above his head.

"She tied one end of the rope to the door handle and made a noose in the other end, then she got that little table over there, in the corner, and put it under the hook, and stood on it, and looped the noose around her neck."

"You mean she –?" he swallowed with difficulty, staring at the old woman. She smiled and looked up at the hook, and in the fire glow he saw a red line across her throat.

"It was the voices, you see. They told her to do it. She could never resist the voices."

He stood slowly, staring at her in fascination.

"That's a hell of a ghost story. Well, I better get to bed. My girlfriend's waiting for me."

"You're in my bedroom," she said, her fingers never ceasing to dart in little insect movements as she clicked her needles.

"What? You should have said something. We could have slept down here in front of the fire."

"It doesn't matter, young man. I welcome the warmth, you know."

The old bitch was really starting to creep him out. He took a step and swayed perilously as the room slowly spun, then stabilized.

"I have to get upstairs," he murmured. "My girlfriend will wonder what happened to me."

"No, she won't."

"What? What do you mean?"

"She's dead," the old woman said simply. "They're all dead up there. Dead and cold in their beds."

She must be suffering from some form of dementia, he thought.

"Well, good-night."

He edged past her chair, unable to take his eyes off her.

He could still hear the click of her knitting needles as he climbed the stairs and went into the room Kim had assigned to him and Sue. The first thing he did was bolt the door. He didn't want that demented old woman coming in with her knitting needles.

It was dark in the bedroom, but the night sky had a kind of funny purple glow that must have been due to the passing thunder storm. It was enough to keep from bumping into the furniture. Sue was already fast asleep. He whispered her name but she didn't respond. Undressing to his boxer shorts, he slid into the bed. The cotton sheets were as cold as ice. He slid across nearer to Sue.

Her back felt as cold as the sheet against his shoulder. He wondered how she could sleep without shivering. Listening, he tried to hear her breaths but there was only silence. The thunder had stopped, and the wind had died down to nothing.

He shivered, and realized his arms and legs were covered in goose bumps. It was freezing in the bed. Jason wondered if he should look around the house for another blanket, then decided what he needed was some body heat. Turning his body, he slid against Sue's icy back and buttocks and put his arm over her waist under the covers. She was naked, which was strange because she usually slept in an undershirt.

Everything about her body felt strange. It was shorter, smaller than he remembered, and the skin was not as smooth. She shifted against him, pressing her wrinkled cheek to his face.

"I like the warmth," she said in his ear.

Stifling the scream that rose in his throat, he tumbled backward from the bed to the floor and scrambled to his feet. He ran from the room and slammed the door shut behind him, then stood in the hall holding onto the door knob with both hands, his heart hammering in his chest. After a few moments, he released the knob and ran down the hall to the room where his friends were sleeping.

The coppery smell of blood filled his nose when he opened the door. He slipped and fell into something sticky, put his palm into it, then rubbed it between his fingers. It was too dark to see it. Something lay against his leg. Without thinking, he reached to push it away. It was soft and cold. He picked it up and felt it with his other hand. Felt five fingers, one by one.

Scrambling upright in the ichor, he ran out and down the stairs. The embers of the fire still glowed, painting the room with a deep red. He approached the fire stiffly, unable to make his legs work as they should, and saw a shadow hanging from the ceiling. It swung back and forth, back and forth. As he got nearer to the fireplace, it resolved itself into the body of a woman, hanging by her neck from a rope.

Slowly the body turned on the rope, revealing its face. Its eyes were open, and its tongue stuck out at the corner of its mouth.

"Sue." He breathed her name without being aware of it.

The eyes closed and opened, and the tongue licked bloodless lips.

"Come back to bed," it said in the old woman's voice.

FALSE IMAGE

“Guess what – I'm being photographed by Nevil Redburn.”

“You're kidding!” Sheena dropped her suitcase and kicked the apartment door shut with her heel. “Nevil Redburn? Jo, that's fantastic.”

Joanne ran over and hugged her roommate.

“I couldn't wait to tell you. At last a real job.”

“How did he contact you? When do you start?”

“Today.” She waved a letter. “His secretary phoned last week, I tried to call you but I couldn't get through.”

The older woman caught the letter out of the air.

“Don't remind me,” she muttered as she read. “Kid, take my advice and never, never do a motorcycle show, I've still got marks from the leather costume they made me wear.”

“You do look beat,” Joanne said. “Sit down and take the load off. I'll put your bag away.”

“Thanks.”

She sat down, then jumped up and began rummaging through the magazine rack beside the sagging sofa.

“What are you looking for?” Joanne said as she came out of the bedroom.

“Redburn, I'm sure we've got one of his around somewhere – oh, here it is. Last month's *Vogue*.”

She pushed a dark curl of hair back from her eye and thumbed the magazine open on the coffee table. Wetting her finger, she flipped the pages.

“There. That's a Redburn piece. Take a look.”

Joanne leaned over her friend's shoulder, It was an advertisement for an expensive perfume. A woman in an evening gown sat languidly on the surface of a black lake, staring down at the reflected image of the moon. The composition was stark, almost harsh, but strangely compelling.

"His secretary said he was looking for a new face. He spotted my portfolio at one of the agencies."

"What's the job?" Sheena murmured.

Both continued to stare at the photograph.

"Some Italian designer. I've never heard of him, but naturally I agreed."

"Naturally."

Sheena tore her eyes away and shut the magazine, looking at Joanne with a smile.

"Looks like I finally get the whole apartment to myself. I hope I can afford it."

"What are you talking about?" Joanne laughed uneasily. "I'm not moving out, It's just a job."

"It's more than that. You're on your way, kid. Once Redburn uses you, every agency in the country will want you."

Joanne shivered and hugged herself. "Even if that were true," she said, eyes shining, "it will still be the same between us. We're buddies."

"Sure." Sheena looked away and kicked off her heels. She stood up and stretched, stifling a yawn.

"I'm so tired I could sleep for a week."

"Not until we celebrate," said a voice from the doorway.

"George? What are you doing?"

A lanky man with disordered hair bustled into the apartment with a bottle and three long-stemmed glasses gathered between his slender fingers.

"Champagne for Miss Hughes' triumphant return from the Windy City."

"It wasn't a triumph, it was a disaster," Sheena said.

"We'll celebrate anyway. The bottle, as you see, is opened, and if we don't drink it in the next ten minutes it will go flat."

"How did you know I was here?"

"I heard the pitter-pat of your fairy feet on my ceiling."

"You're the only one with fairy feet," Joanne said.

"Shrew. You cut me to the core."

In a few minutes they were seated around the battered coffee table, Joanne on the rug, Sheena and George on the sofa. Joanne had set out crackers with cheese. Sheena was voraciously devouring them one after another.

"I suppose," she said between bites, "Jo's told you the news."

The face of the man darkened. He stared at the bubbles in his glass.

Sheena looked inquiringly at Joanne. Joanne arched her brows and shrugged.

"George has got this idea that Redburn is, I don't know, dangerous."

"What?" Sheena asked laughing.

"He doesn't want me to take the assignment."

"What have you got against Redburn, George? Don't tell me he's straight? Jo, I think I hear wedding bells."

"He's evil," George said sullenly. "Let's leave it at that, shall we?"

"Not on your life," said Sheena. "Not until you tell me what you know. Jo, what did he tell you?"

"Nothing – not a word."

George pushed himself to his feet and walked nervously across the floor. When he turned, his long face was serious.

"I don't know anything, exactly, but I've heard stories."

"God, this business lives on gossip," Sheena said.

Ignoring her, George spoke to Joanne.

"There was this girl about a year ago, a model. I didn't know her but I used to see her around the clubs. Nice kid from the Midwest. She got an assignment from Redburn."

The drop in his voice and the pause at the end of his words made both women lean forward unconsciously.

"She disappeared. She went to that house up on the coast where Redburn works and no one ever saw her again."

"There must have been inquiries," said Sheena.

"Why? She was a faceless nobody."

A moment of silence lengthened between them.

"Did you see the work?" Joanne asked.

"Oh yes," George nodded, "Superb. I believe it won several awards in Europe."

"There you are," Sheena said to Joanne. "Even if Redburn was Count

Dracula himself you couldn't afford to pass up this job and you know it."

Joanne topped up her glass with the last of the champagne, draining the bottle. No bubbles fizzed. It was already flat.

"She's right, George. I told you. I have to go, whatever stories you've heard."

"Don't you think he knows that?" George pressed. He knelt on the rug beside her and took her cold hand in his. "He's a spider and you're the fly."

She carefully extracted her hand and looked at her watch.

"I have to get ready. Redburn's chauffeur is picking me up at eight."

"A night shoot," Sheena said. "He must be the temperamental artsy type."

"At least let us come with you," George said, following her into the bedroom.

"No. The secretary was very explicit. No hangers-on. Redburn hates anyone under foot."

"Any witnesses, you mean."

An hour later the blip of a horn in the street signaled the arrival of the car.

Sheena parted the curtains and peered down through the dusty window.

"A Mercedes. Elegant but not ostentatious."

Joanne emerged from the bedroom. Her long blonde hair hung loose, and her face was clean-scrubbed. Redburn would have his own makeup artist and hair stylist. Without paint, her face was childlike and vulnerable.

"Well," she breathed, "wish me luck. No, don't come down with me, I'm getting right into the car."

Pressing through their chatter and trying to ignore the concerned look George gave her, she shut the apartment door and went down to the street.

The chauffeur was lounging against the fender of the car. A big man with dark skin and waterless black eyes, he pushed himself erect and silently opened the rear door. The car sealed out the city noises as it smoothly merged with the evening traffic.

It was more than an hour's drive from the heart of the city to the isolated oceanfront house where Redburn had his private studio. The house was built on a cantilevered concrete slab that extended into space out from the stony cliff on which it perched. A solid wall of glass fronted the ocean, As they drove along the serpentine drive Joanne could see the soft yellow glow of lights.

The chauffeur escorted her into the foyer and told her to wait, then disappeared back outside. She heard the soft rustle of the car engine and the crunch of its tires on gravel as it drove away. The sound diminished to silence.

She walked across the tiled floor of the entrance hall nervously, purse clutched in both her hands, listening for some sound. There was no place to sit. The chill of the white plaster walls was brightened by a large photographic print of a nude lying face down in a field of poppies. The track lighting in the ceiling drew her attention to it. She studied it, wondering if it was Redburn's own work.

"One of my creations."

Startled, she turned toward the Roman arch that led into a corridor under the sweeping stairs.

A smiling man approached with his hand extended. His tanned face looked about forty but he moved with the strength and grace of a younger man. Coal black hair lay flat against his scalp. His gray eyes captured and held her. She felt her hand taken briefly in his strong grasp.

"Everyone wonders about the print. I suppose vanity makes me display it this way, but I am fond of it."

"It's wonderful – so alive."

"Yes. Would you follow me, Miss Morley? We've been waiting for you. Everything is prepared."

Joanne trailed after him through a large studio into a brightly lit dressing room. Everything looked so normal she forgot her nervousness. The dresses she was to model were hanging from a steel rack. A Japanese woman in a white smock bowed and smiled as they entered.

"This is Nikki, my assistant. She will fix your hair and put on your face."

Joanne sat in the swivel chair before the illuminated mirror and let the deft fingers of the woman flutter about her head. Whatever apprehension she might have felt was submerged in the preoccupations of the job at hand. Murmuring instructions, Nikki helped her into one of the dresses and led her into the studio.

Redburn examined her coolly.

"You'll do," he said, giving her a brief smile of encouragement. "Into the set. Hurry – we've got a lot to do."

His professionalism reassured Joanne. He might work strange hours but he knew exactly what he wanted. With the silent chauffeur operating the lights and the wind machine that stirred the foliage on the tropical set, Redburn moved catlike back and forth in front of her, crouching and kneeling, the winder of the camera whirring in his hands. It was one of his eccentricities that he continued to use film cameras in a digital age. She lost track of time and the costume changes. His strong voice lulled her with an almost hypnotic quality.

"Time for a break," he said at last. "We don't want to wear you out."

Joanne looked past him at the clock on the studio wall and realized she had been modeling for more than two hours. With that realization, she felt the tremor of her fatigue and gratefully stepped out of the set.

Nikki carried in coffee from another room and vanished. The chauffeur was nowhere to be seen.

"You are tired, aren't you?" he said with concern.

"No – not really."

"Yes you are. I could feel your vitality draining away, I can't have that. The next series is critical. The coffee will pick you up."

She looked down at her half-empty cup, sudden doubt flitting through her mind.

"No drugs," he said, laughing. "I don't believe in them. Nikki's something of a herbalist."

She smiled warmly, disarmed by his direct manner.

"I'm afraid I've been behaving foolishly," she said.

"It's all right, I know my methods are unconventional. And I suppose you've heard stories."

She stared at him, not knowing how to answer.

"Yes, I see you have. Do you know what prompts them? Jealousy. My competitors envy my success."

"They have reason to be jealous."

"You flatter me."

"No, really. Your pictures are so alive. When I look at them I almost expect the models to get up and walk."

"Shall I tell you my secret?" he asked, his eyes challenging her.

She did not know if he was serious.

"But perhaps it would bore you."

"On the contrary, I'd be fascinated."

"Good. Come with me."

She put her empty coffee cup down and followed him through a side door into a darkroom. The overhead light was on. He shut the door behind her.

"What do you know about subliminal advertising?" he asked, crouching before a filing cabinet and opening the bottom drawer.

"Not much. Wasn't it tried in movie houses in the nineteen-fifties to sell popcorn?"

"And other things."

He pulled a print from the drawer and carried it to a cork board on the wall, where he pinned it up. Then he busied himself with a projector.

"It was banned," she went on as she watched him. "The government never proved that it worked, but they considered it too dangerous to ignore."

"Did you know that subliminal messages are in modern magazine advertising?"

"I've heard rumors but nobody's admitting it."

"It's there, believe me."

He drew two 35mm film negatives from different drawers of a negative file and put one into the projector.

"Is that what you use? Some kind of subliminal message?"

"Here, look at this," he said, pulling her close with his arm around her shoulder.

She looked at his face. There was a strange tension in his voice.

On the flat white surface below the projector was the pale image of the negative. Redburn reached over the counter and dimmed the overhead lights by turning a small switch. Joanne recognized a picture of a woman standing on top of a marble pillar from a Greek temple. The colors were all wrong and the light and dark areas inverted, but she was well enough accustomed to negative images to have no difficulty making out the scene.

"Now watch."

He inserted the second negative into the projector above the first. The result was two images superimposed. At first Joanne could not separate the second picture. Then she did and felt her stomach twist in disgust.

On the dress of the model in the first picture was the figure of a starving black child. It sat peering out pitifully, its skin stretched across its skull-like head and its swollen belly bulging over its stick legs.

"This is one of my early works. I've refined the technique considerably in the last few years. But this was the seed."

"It's horrible." Joanne said involuntarily.

"Why?" he asked in genuine surprise. "You've seen images like this before. People use them to get what they want. Charities. The news media. Politicians. I've just done the same thing in a different way."

Joanne stared at the enlarged stomach of the infant and suppressed her revulsion.

"You mean all your pictures have something like this hidden inside them?"

"They all have subliminal imaging. I'll show you. Look at the print on the board."

Joanne turned and realized that the photograph Redburn had pinned to the wall was the same one of the model on the pillar. But there was no trace of the child. She went to it and touched its surface.

"The eye sees more than the conscious mind realizes," Redburn said. "Under ordinary yellow light it's invisible. But through a special filter – watch."

The room dimmed to an unearthly violet. The wailing child seemed to leap out of the photograph at Joanne. She took a step back, her insides sick, her thoughts churning. Her hand went to her mouth.

"Will my photographs have images like this hidden in them?" she asked softly.

"Of course not," he said in a brisk tone. "I told you this was a preliminary stage. I've progressed far beyond it."

She felt a faint relief.

"But what – ?"

"Come along, Miss Morley. I've wasted enough time. I'm sure you're rested now. It's a failing I have, talking about my work, and I tend to overindulge myself."

Once again his voice was coolly professional. She wondered if he felt insulted by her lack of enthusiasm. If so, he did not show it. He held the door of the darkroom open for her to pass.

She emerged into the bright studio and stopped. The tropical set had been replaced by one of a wooden scaffold with ropes and pulleys against a blood red backdrop. To one side an iron charcoal brazier glowed. Nikki stood before it turning long rods that rested with their ends buried in the coals. They looked like iron bars. The Japanese woman noticed her attention and smiled politely.

"We've completed the preliminary shooting," Redburn explained. "Now I need the subliminal images that will vitalize the final prints. Miss Morley, I'm afraid I will have to ask you to remove all your clothes."

She broke from his touch and ran for the door. The chauffeur caught her by the wrists and brutally began removing her dress.

"Careful, Karl, we don't want the gown damaged. Nikki, help him."

The woman left the brazier and helped the dark man strip Joanne. They dragged her to the scaffold and bound her wrists over her head.

Nikki took one of the rods out of the fire. Its end glowed yellow-white. A thin wisp of smoke curled from it. She brought the bar close to Joanne's cheek.

Joanne stared at it blankly, her body slack with shock. She could not even turn away. The heat of the iron felt like warm sunshine on her face.

Redburn picked up his camera and looped its strap over his neck.

"Come now, Miss Morley," he said in annoyance. "You are a professional. I want to see real horror in your eyes. Do you think you can manage that?"

Joanne looked at him, seeing him clearly through the dull haze of her emotions, and her face twisted.

He nodded.

"All right. Nikki, you may begin."

THE IVORY BOX

The Lady Soo Lin gazed into the burnished silver circle of her hand mirror and studied with fatalistic despair the fine spider webs radiating from her fathomless dark eyes. Not even the heavy white paint currently in fashion at the Imperial Court could fill them.

For the first time she forced herself to acknowledge that she had lost the favor of the Emperor. True, he spoke no slighting word, gave no sign of disapproval, but of late when he pressed her to his breast, it was with the casual indifference one displayed toward a useful but worn object, not the passion of an ardent lover. No longer was she summoned to his chamber nightly to teach his youthful mind undreamt delights. Now younger women passed her on their way to the ruler's door, their eyes turning to her with quick flickers of disdain.

Determination hardened the reflected white mask. She had not devoted her life to learning the secrets of love only to be supplanted by mindless, plump bodies. Not she, who had reigned supreme in her art for decades, the greatest living courtesan, her single destiny the pleasing of men.

Soo Lin felt no rancor toward the Emperor. It was the nature of men to seek novelty. What he learned from her experienced hands and lips he delighted to teach the innocent young children of the palace. Yet she vowed to fight with all her wiles to keep what was hers, with sorcery if she must. She smiled her bitterness. It would not be the first time a potion or charm revived the flagging ardor of a bored lover.

She picked from her table a small chest of ivory. It was little larger than the flat of her hand and plain save for certain arcane symbols carved in its lid. When she turned it, something rattled inside. Opening the clasp, she took out a vial of greenish liquid and concealed it in her sable hair.

She had kept the box hidden near her for three long weeks while she waited for his summons, every day fearing its discovery. The act she contemplated was treason, its punishment death by slow torture. At last the call had come. The Emperor waited for her now in his bedchamber.

With trembling fingers she slid the ivory box into the wide sleeve of her blue silk gown and counted the painful, mincing steps down the corridor to the chamber of her lover. Like all high-born women, her feet had been bound shortly after birth to lend them the childlike delicacy men so much admired. The bones were bent and twisted from their sockets, making each step a stab of pain. Soo Lin betrayed nothing behind her carefully painted mask, neither the familiar ache nor the anguish of her anticipation.

He lay lounging on silk pillows, his golden robe indolently open to reveal the near-whiteness of his skin. Plumes of incense curled in sensuous pearling ripples to the gilded ceiling. Languidly he gestured for her to pour him wine, as he always did. Though still young, he was a man of habit.

She knelt at a low table and emptied clear wine from a crystal vessel into his shallow golden cup. Secretly she risked a glance at him from the corner of her black-lined eye. He lay staring at the smoke that floated across the ceiling, face slack with drug-induced stupor. Her shaking hand drew the vial from her hair and emptied the greenish oil into the wine. Once dispersed through the cup, the tint was hardly noticeable. Neither was there any odor to betray its presence.

She knelt on the dragon-patterned rug beside the Emperor's couch and raised the cup in both hands. He took it with barely a glance at her bowed head and ordered her to sing.

Long custom had taught her the songs he favored when in a melancholy and pensive mood, as he was this night. She sang in a quiet voice a lulling air without accompaniment.

"I have been unkind to you, Little Flower," he murmured, stroking her hair. "You must not believe I love you less than the others, for only you can rescue me from the windowless corridors of my soul."

She smiled the appropriate degree with the corners of her red lips. Again she sang, this time about the mild pleasures of the garden in early morning light. The hum of bees was in her voice and the graceful flight of swallows.

The cup slipped from his lax fingers and struck the thick rug noiselessly. His breaths became long and deep.

Breaking off her song, she crept to his side and studied his pale face with darting, nervous glances. He slept as one drugged with opium, his chest rising and falling in shallow sighs, but seemed unhurt. Relieved, she drew the ivory casket from the sleeve of her gown and held it near her body as she looked around the chamber. There was no assured secrecy this close to the royal person. Even the shadows might hold watchful eyes.

What had the traveling monk said? She must give her lover the potion, then when his sleeping breath turned white, catch it in the ivory box. Thereafter, so long as the box remained safely locked, he would torment her with the excess of his passion.

She hesitated. Almost she wavered in her purpose, so painful in her memory were the gentle words of the Emperor. Perhaps he did care for her still, and would return when the novelty of round young limbs faded. She steeled her resolve. Words were only words, and would not erase the lines of age from her face in the chill morning light after loving words were long forgotten.

Heart hammering at her treasonable presumption, she lifted the hem of her gown and slid her lithe body along the bare thighs of the sleeping man, then worked herself forward on her knees until she straddled his naked, heaving chest. She held the ivory box between her delicate hands and waited.

Soon the face of the Emperor began to sweat and jerk as though he were locked in the throes of a nightmare. His breath came shudderingly with soft moans of despair, and she felt the thud of his heart beneath her. A whitish mist appeared from his nostrils and gathered densely over his face. It was much like the smoke of the incense sticks, save that it did not rise and seemed to pulse as though possessed of life.

A terrible exultation thrilled through the slight body of the courtesan as she stared wide-eyed at the strange white mist. She felt herself to be balanced on the edge of an abyss. The next step would plunge her irrevocably into a fate she could not foresee. At the same time she thrilled with illicit power. Beneath her thighs lay the master of the world, yet in moments he would be a slave to her love.

As the monk had instructed, she waited until a large white cloud formed and the Emperor's breaths came in ragged gasps. Then she shifted her knees against his chest and leaned forward, holding the open ivory casket close to his face while chanting words in a strange language that meant nothing to her, but which she had learned by rote.

The weight of her knees forced a deep groan from the Emperor. A dense mist issued from his nose and mouth and was drawn as if by some unfelt draft into the ivory box. When the last of the mist passed under the lid, the courtesan snapped it shut and locked the silver clasp.

It was done. He would be her passionate slave for as long as the box remained safe. Soo Lin intended to guard it with her life. She rose from the couch and hid the box under a towel so he would not see it when he awoke. Turning, she stifled a cry. For a moment a black shadow lengthened across the sleeping form of the Emperor. As it faded, he opened his eyes and sat up, regarding her without blinking. Then he gestured for her to approach.

Fighting tears of fierce joy, Soo Lin ran to his couch and fell into his embrace. His arms were strangely powerful around her and the unexpected passion in his kiss left her breathless. Wordlessly he stripped away her garments and made love to her with savage force.

Her smooth back ran red where his fingernails raked, and her white arms and buttocks bruised under his rough touch. Pitiless with desire, he struck her thighs apart and crushed her beneath him, stabbing her body with inflamed lust, torturing her with exquisite agonies.

She endured her injuries in silence. It was not her place to complain. Was it not her body the Emperor sought? And was that not all she had ever longed for?

Three times that night he took her, and twice on the early morrow before he permitted her to rise. For the first time in months Soo Lin felt truly happy. The aching of her bruised limbs was unimportant. No other woman had ever evoked such passion from the bored young ruler. This she knew to be so, for the ladies of the court talked of their adventures among themselves. Though, in truth, the brutal hunger on his sculptured features was almost unseemly in one of highest birth. Frowning, she pushed this unworthy thought aside.

As she bent to pick up the towel that hid the ivory box, she felt a prickling along her spine and turned. The Emperor sat watching her from his couch, his strangely glittering eyes not on her, but on the bundle in her hands. A mocking smile fleeted across his pale lips.

"Leave that," he said in a voice that creaked like a dry cart wheel.

"It is soiled," she murmured, head bowed.

"No matter – put it down." His words held the edge of command.

Clumsy with fear, she unwrapped the box and set the towel down. His eyes bored into the ivory lid as she tried to hide it behind her fluttering hands.

"What is that toy?" he asked.

"A poor thing of little value."

The Emperor smiled again and motioned her nearer. She crept forward, her body trembling. He pulled her roughly to his side and kissed her. Flinching back with an involuntary shudder at his savagery, she tasted the salt of her own blood where his teeth had cut her lower lip.

"Since it is so poor a thing, you will not regret giving it to me."

He extended his pallid hand with the palm up.

To refuse the wish of the Emperor was unthinkable. She offered the ivory casket at arm's length. He struggled to take it from her hands, but could not. Some unseen barrier barred his touch. She drew it back and held it close to her breast.

The fury of the Emperor momentarily took away his speech. Soo Lin watched his body melt and twist as if some misshapen shape struggled within it. She stared into his black eyes, twin mirrors of volcanic glass, and knew this was not the man she loved but a demon wearing his flesh. She recalled the dark shadow and shrank farther away from him.

Deception dropped from his face like a trap door opened on the fires of hell. He stood from the couch and stared brazenly at her, taunting her, while his naked body writhed with obscene vitality. In some perverse way Soo Lin knew she was confronting, not her lover, but her rival.

"Place the box into my hand," he growled. "Once I have destroyed it, I will raise an army of wolves from this land of sheep and conquer the world, and you shall rule beside me."

The full horror of what she had done at last dawned upon Soo Lin. Within the small ivory casket lay the very soul of the Emperor, the gentle dreaming man she wanted only to love, yet she had betrayed him more foully than the cruelest assassin. For a moment overcome by pity, she pressed the box to her heart and rocked it like a dead child.

Her back stiffened. She was born of a philosopher class which taught that life was worth nothing unless lived truly. She stepped forward with a deep bow that the demon pretended to acknowledge. Bringing the box almost within his grasp, she tore it open and threw it at the demon's lusting face.

An inhuman shriek issued from his throat as the white mist boiled from the casket and engulfed him. He fell writhing to the marble tiles. A strange battle of light and shadow played over his limbs. The face that had once smiled with such melancholy sadness twisted with the agonies of fire and ice, and foam flecked the Emperor's finely chiseled features. His back arched like a drawn bow. A dark fume boiled from his ears and nostrils and fled across the room like a shadow driven before the sun.

The Emperor collapsed and lay breathing heavily for so long a time that Soo Lin thought he had fallen into a swoon; then he raised himself on his arm and looked about with a dazed expression. Slowly he gained his feet. He swayed like a man newly recovered from near fatal illness.

Soo Lin cried aloud her joy and ran to kneel humbly at her ruler's feet, eyes lowered, heart prepared to receive whatever chastisement he might give. She felt his gentle fingers on her shoulders and smiled through her tears, for she recognized the familiar touch of her lover. Whatever her fate, the evil she had inadvertently evoked had failed and been driven back to the outer darkness.

Her smile became a grimace as the long white fingers tightened around her throat. Forcing her head up, she peered through the blackness advancing across her sight into the eyes of the Emperor, and learned the final tragedy of her life. The soul of the Emperor had reclaimed its body, but the price of its victory was utter madness.

GOING TO SEE MR. WINTERS

The woman bunched the front of her coat tight against the dusty October wind. A sheet of yesterday's newspaper danced around her head and pressed against her side, then flew off laughing into the darkness of the empty street. She took no notice. Her eyes were on the yellow light cast from the newsstand at the corner. They were pinched black eyes that reached out from a face of wax, contracting all hope into two tiny darting points.

The newsdealer sat on a stool in the back of his booth, smoking a cigar. The upper part of his face lay in shadow – only his thick mouth and the short fingers of the hand that rubbed his chin were visible.

"Wanna buy a paper?" he said, running the words together indifferently.

"I want to see Mr. Winters. They –" she pointed vaguely the way she had come "– told me you knew how."

Rubber lips parted on tobacco-yellow teeth.

"I don't know nothin'. I sell papers – you wanna paper?"

She looked around her, blinking painfully at the dented trash cans, the peeling paint, the sooty red brick walls. A train whistle blew from nowhere.

"Yes, I'll buy a paper." Taking from the pocket of her coat a worn leather change purse and peering close, not looking at him: "They told me you could help me, they said you knew how I could reach Mr. Winters –"

"This paper's special. Cost you extra."

She held her breath an imperceptible moment.

"How much extra?"

"Twenty."

73

"All right."

He handed her the paper. She set the bill down and he pinned it before the wind took it away.

"Take a look across the street. See that dwarf with the shoeshine case by the alley there? Been around a long time. He knows things. Go talk to him."

She searched the dusty shadows. Beside a block of darkness sat a little rumpled pile of clothes. She turned back to the dealer, but the newsstand was shut and its light was out.

"I'm looking for Mr. Winters," she said.

The motionless pile at her feet stirred, took on shape. An old felt hat slowly tilted, and a sin-lined child's face smiled.

"If I take you, there's no way back," it whispered.

"I know."

"Cost you fifty," it said, looking away.

"I haven't got fifty."

"What have you got?"

She told.

"Give it."

"What about –?"

"Him?" The dwarf shrugged. "He don't want nothin'."

Getting up slowly, it shook the dust from the seams of its baggy trousers. A tiny white hand slid out of a coat sleeve.

"It's dark – hold on."

She reached for the hand, trembled and drew back.

"Take it," the dwarf snapped.

It was cold on her fingers, moving and tightening sightlessly against her as it drew her into the mouth of the alley.

Parked beneath a street lamp was a black limousine, its engine rustling softly, its lights dimmed. Closed blinds hid the interior of the rear compartment. The black driver sat behind the wheel looking straight ahead. With the nail of his index finger, the dwarf tapped three times respectfully against the glass. The window slid down on electric silence.

"She wants to see him," said the dwarf.

The driver gauged her worn clothes, the hollows of her cheeks, the emptiness of her eyes.

"Wait."

He closed the window and spoke into a microphone, eyes flashing white at the corners as he glanced at her, responding to unheard questions. The dwarf began to inch away, fading into the darkness – when she turned from the black man's cynical gaze, she was alone on the curb.

The driver stood beside the open rear door, mutely inviting her to step inside. He shut the door discretely after her, then re-entered the front. The car began to move. The interior was dim; she felt more than saw the bulk of the figure beside her.

"I'm Winters," he said distantly. "What is it you want?"

"I –" Her mouth betrayed her, would not form her thoughts.

"You needn't be embarrassed. Nothing you say will go further."

His tone was dryly informal; that of a businessman with a client.

She did not speak.

"Do you know what my service consists of?"

"Yes," she said quickly. "Of course."

He took a cigarette from a small gold case that glittered and flashed in his hand, lit it. His movements were relaxed.

"Perhaps you have a problem you'd like to discuss?"

A pane of glass isolated them from the driver. Through the front windscreen came the moving lights of the city, casting green and purple shadows on the plush upholstery.

She began to talk, hesitantly at first, about her life, the emptiness, the pain, the need for money. She spoke about one person's illness, another's desertion, the words breaking forth uncontrolled, her longing, her desire, her hopes, her cares, tumbling out with frantic vitality, always returning to money, money, the bridge across her many sufferings. He listened without interruption, inhaling her words with the smoke of his cigarette deep into his lungs. When she was done, he nodded slowly.

"You've tried to help yourself, I suppose?"

"Yes." Her cheeks were wet with weary tears. She wiped them away. "I haven't the strength –"

"I understand. You were right to come to me."

"There's nothing I can pay you with."

He motioned her to silence almost angrily.

"My work is its own reward. I consider myself a servant of the public."

Butting his cigarette in the ashtray, he pressed a button on the panel before him. The driver acknowledged the signal through the glass and braked the car to the side of the road. He sat with his gloved hands on the wheel, not turning around, waiting.

"Get out," Winters told her.

She unlatched the door and stepped onto the damp earth. There were woods all around, black trunks of trees that rose motionless in the stillness. The narrow strip of road wandered in two directions and was lost. She walked slowly into the trees. Behind she heard the crack of Winter's shoe against a twig, and turned. He was silhouetted against the glow from the open door, perhaps ten yards away from her.

"Kneel."

The ground was wet on her legs through the material of her coat. She saw him take something from his pocket and hold it up.

"Repeat after me," he said. "I forgive your act of mercy…"

"I forgive your act of mercy…"

"… and bless you for it."

"… and bless you for it."

"Amen."

"Amen."

There was a flash of silence.

A LEAF FROM THE COTTONIAN GENESIS

1.

Eleanor Hartley went to a window and peered into the night. All she could see was snow falling past the glass. The outer darkness turned the window into a black mirror. She heard a crackle of sparks and watched the shadowy reflection of her host as he bent to stir logs in the fireplace with a poker.

"Shouldn't the others be here by now?"

He shrugged. "Maybe they started late, and got caught by the snow."

"I barely got up here myself. It was just starting to build up on the road when I reached the base of the mountain."

"If they stop at *Sam's Gas*, he'll put chains on their tires. They'll make it."

"I sure hope so," she said, sipping white wine from her glass.

If not, she would be here alone overnight in this mountain chalet with a man she hardly knew. David Kline was wealthy, a friend of several of her society friends. He was charming, witty, and well-dressed, but somehow she had not become comfortable with him, even though he was frequently at the same events she attended. Maybe it was his age – he was twice as old as the crowd he liked to socialize with. His watery blue eyes were so pale, they made her skin creep every time he looked at her.

"If they don't make it tonight, they'll be here by tomorrow morning. The road gets plowed regularly. I wouldn't have bought this place if I couldn't count on access to the city."

She had agreed to spend the weekend at Kline's mountain home on the promise of the best downhill skiing in Colorado. An old friend from her private Catholic school days, Kathy Channing, had invited her, assuring her that three or four other people she knew would be there. Now here she was, and the dense falling snow beyond the window made it unlikely that anyone else would arrive at least until the following day.

Not that she was seriously worried about her host's intentions. He had always displayed impeccable manners. The gray hair at his temples gave him a scholarly appearance. She vaguely remembered being told that he was a collector of some kind. He had made a great deal of money in business, and now he was retired and a patron of the Colorado art scene. Or so she had been informed by someone, where or when she could not remember. Several times in the past month she had noticed him among the crowd in the modern art gallery she managed.

She wandered around the rustic living room, which took up the entire front half of the chalet. The exterior walls were massive pine logs chinked together with white mortar. Slanting oak beams textured to look as though they had been hewn with a broad axe divided the white panels of the cathedral ceiling. The reflected glow from the stone fireplace on the pine floor was interrupted only by a white sheepskin rug in front of the hearth. A broad oak staircase led up to a railed landing that ran the full width of the room. It must have cost him at least five million, she thought.

Here and there, on the walls and tables, were objects she presumed to be part of David's art collection. He seemed to favor religious art from before the Renaissance. It was not her period of interest. She wondered what had drawn him into her gallery? There were framed pages of illuminated manuscripts, Russian icons of the Virgin Mary, elaborate crucifixes in gold and silver. None of it was her kind of art. She pretended not to notice him watching her as he puttered with the fire.

On the wall to the left of the fireplace hung a small painting in an ornately carved frame of ebony. Below it was a plain table, and on either end of the table stood tall silver candle sticks with thick, white church candles. The candles were not lit, but the way they framed the painting gave it a curious emphasis that drew her over. It resembled a kind of shrine.

"May I refresh your glass?"

"Please."

She studied the painting. It looked very old, although its subject had nothing sacred about it. A naked male figure stood in profile with his right leg advanced, his right arm raised as though imploring or cursing heaven. His other arm hung down in front of his groin, partly concealing it. Dark fire seemed to coruscate up and down the surface of his skin, and flames rose from his black hair. He stood on the brink of a cliff, and behind him huge tumbled rocks formed an impenetrable wall. The artist had captured the figure just as he was turning his head to look out from the painting.

When Eleanor's gaze met the glaring eyes of the figure, she felt a shock run through her body. The expression on the handsome but brutal face was raw rage, a kind of aristocratic arrogance, and something more. It took her a moment to recognize what it was. Desire – no, not desire, lust.

She smelled David's aftershave before she realized he was beside her. He steadied her hand while he refilled her glass with wine from the bottle, then released her fingers.

"What do you think?"

She continued to study the painting.

"It's powerful."

"Yes, it is," he agreed. "That was my first impression of it when I saw it at the dealer's in Manhattan."

"You collect paintings?"

"I mainly collect illustrated manuscript pages. This is a page from a book, you know. The monks who copied religious texts by hand would illustrate them with pictures."

"It looks old."

"Sixth century, or maybe even earlier. It has an interesting history, if you'd like to hear it."

"I would."

"I always ask, you know, because some people are bored when I talk about my collection, and I know the art of the Dark Ages is not your area of expertise."

With her left hand, she toyed with the silver cross that hung between her breasts, waiting for him to go on.

"This is an illuminated page from a Greek manuscript called the

Cottonian Genesis. Nobody knows who created it or where, but some believe the manuscript was made at Alexandria, in Egypt, by Christian monks. Its text was the text of the first book of the Bible, but what made this manuscript especially interesting was the number of paintings it contained. There were hundreds of them, mostly miniature paintings that illustrated various aspects of the story of creation."

"Were?"

"The manuscript was destroyed by fire in 1731."

She studied the painting. There were no traces of fire damage. He laughed softly.

"I'll get to that. The first solid information about the manuscript surfaced when it was given as a gift to King Henry VIII of England by two bishops visiting England from Philippi, in Greece. From Henry it went on to his daughter, Elizabeth the First, who gave it to one of her tutors, Sir John Fortescue, who gave it to Sir Robert Cotton."

"Hence the name, Cottonian Genesis," she said.

"Exactly. Robert Cotton was one of the great book collectors of England. For a time his library was kept in Ashburnham House in Westminster, a borough of London. In 1731 a fire broke out. That was a common danger in those times, when rooms were heated by fireplaces and lighted with candles. Anyway, some of the books in the Cotton collection were damaged in the fire, and one of the worst damaged was the Cottonian Genesis. All we have left today are charred fragments of a few dozen pages, mostly with text on them, along with a few badly damaged illustrations. The great manuscript, one of the most important manuscripts in European history, was almost totally destroyed."

"And yet?" she said, pointing at the painting.

"That's the interesting part of the story," he said, smiling. "While the manuscript was in possession of Queen Elizabeth, she lent it to her astrologer, Dr. John Dee. For some reason – nobody knows why he did it – Dee tore out one of the few full-page illustrations in the work and kept it for himself. That's the rumor, anyway. There is no mention of the theft in official historical documents, so it's possible nobody ever noticed it was missing."

"When did this happen?"

"Some time in the late 16th century."

"So the painting was already gone when the manuscript was destroyed in the fire."

"Exactly. Here, let me show you something."

Setting down his wine glass, he carefully removed the painting from the wall and turned it over. The back was not solid, but a sheet of glass that exposed the back of the vellum manuscript leaf. On it was drawn in black ink a curious pentacle of a double circle inside a double square tipped on its corner. Strange letters ran around the circle between its two lines, and similar letters filled each side of the square. A scorch mark ran across both circle and square in the lower corner. It looked almost as though someone had carelessly laid a cigarette down and forgotten it.

"Can you read it?" she asked.

"In a manner of speaking. I know what the letters are. They are from a magical alphabet called Enochian that Dee is supposed to have received through a crystal ball from the angels of heaven. Unfortunately, I don't know what they mean. I haven't been able to decipher what they say."

"What's this?" She pointed at a small mark in one corner of the pentacle. It was a tiny upright triangle.

"That's Dee's signature. Delta, for Dee, get it? The Greek letter Delta is shaped like a triangle."

"It's too bad it was damaged. But it couldn't have been done in the fire."

"No, that happened much later."

He hung the picture back on its hook. The glaring eyes of the figure met hers and made her blink. It reminded her a little bit of William Blake's painting *The Ghost of a Flea*.

"Is this supposed to be the Devil?"

"The folklore surrounding the picture says not. It is the portrait of one of the beings set by God to watch over the world." He glanced at her cross. "You're a Catholic girl. How well do you know your Bible?"

"Well enough, I guess. It was drummed into us by nuns."

"Then you remember that in the sixth chapter of Genesis, mention is made of angelic beings called the Sons of God, who looked down upon the earth and lusted after the daughters of humanity. In the book of Enoch they are called Watchers. They made a pact between themselves to descend to the earth and sire children on mortal women. Their offspring became great heroes and "mighty men," as the Bible puts it. The Watchers stayed with their mortal wives and taught humanity all kinds of forbidden arts and sciences. When God found out what was going on, he was so furious he banished all the Watchers to an abyss of endless shadow, and caused the Great Flood that washed humanity away – all except Noah and his family who were safe on the ark."

"Is this supposed to be one of the Watchers?"

"This is Semjaza, who is said in the book of Enoch to be have been their leader."

She made herself meet the eyes of the burning figure in the painting. The flames seemed to crawl along the surface of his skin like sensuous red and black serpents.

"So he's the one who convinced the others to disobey God."

"I suppose so," David murmured.

"He's a fallen angel."

"Some of the stories surrounding the painting say he's not really an angel at all, but one of the djinn. According to Islamic lore, the djinn are fire spirits ranked between angels and men who are independent of God's will."

"Why would God set djinn to be Watchers over the earth?"

"I don't know – maybe because it was an office that was beneath the dignity of the true angels."

"He must have enjoyed his work."

"What do you mean?"

She pointed between the legs of the figure. It was possible to just make out on either side of the dangling left wrist that the flame-lined phallus of the spirit was engorged and erect.

"I'll be damned," he said, staring at the painting. "Do you know, I never noticed that. You have a good eye."

He rested his hand lightly on her shoulder. She glanced over at him, but he was studying the painting intently, or pretending to. After a moment, she slid away.

It was not the first time she had been in this situation, alone with a man who was attracted to her, but it was always awkward. She couldn't afford to allow the scenario to progress, since there was no way she could drive down the winding mountain in this snow. She was trapped here.

She took out her phone, hit Cathy's number, then frowned as she listened. No connection, only a kind of static hiss. She tried the numbers of two others David had told her were coming when he had invited her to the chalet a week ago, but the result was the same.

"I don't believe the others are coming," she said.

"What do you mean?" There was a trace of sharpness in his tone.

"I mean, I don't see how they can get up the road with all this snow."

He relaxed slightly. "No matter. We'll have the house to ourselves tonight, and they'll be here tomorrow morning."

For the first time, she wondered if anyone else actually was coming? She dismissed the notion, but it clung to the edge of her thoughts. Suppose he had cancelled the weekend for all but her? But that would be crazy.

The lights went out, and the soft tinkle of a jazz piano that had been playing on the turntable in the corner gave way to the crackle of burning wood in the fireplace.

"Don't be alarmed," he said. "It's one of the hazards to living on a mountain road. In heavy weather the power sometimes fails. It's usually not out for more than a few hours."

She watched as he went around, lighting candles that were positioned at various places in the room for just such an emergency. He lit the two white candles on either side of the painting in the black frame. Their flickering light animated the figure of Semjaza so that it seemed alive.

"I'll open another bottle of wine. If you like, we can play a game to pass the time. Do you play chess?"

As he turned, she saw that the front of his pants were domed out by a distinct erection. Whether or not he noticed the direction of her gaze, he kept his back to her as he went to a cupboard to get out a folding chess board.

"David, I'm very tired and I have a headache. I'm not used to so much wine. I'd really just like to go to bed. Would you show me my room?"

He stopped and cocked his head as though listening to some inner voice, then put the board away.

"Of course. How inconsiderate of me. I'll get you a candle and show you to the room. Your bag is already in there. The well pump runs on electricity, but I'm sure there will be enough pressure left for you to wash and brush."

2.

Something woke her from dreamless sleep. She listened to the silence, lying motionless. The bedroom David had assigned to her was dimly lit by a pale sky glow that found its way through the window. A fitful gust threw a sift of snow across the glass.

Blinking dryness from her eyes, she found her phone and studied its screen. It was just after midnight. No sounds came from the rest of the house. David must be asleep in one of the other bedrooms. She eased out of bed and slung a quilted robe over her silk pyjamas. Cinching it tight at the waist, she slid her feet into slippers, then crossed to the door and pressed her ear against it. Nothing. She was relieved to find the bolt still in place. No one could open the door from the outside by stealth.

She started back to bed, but some impulse made her pause and return to the door. She slid the bolt and opened it. The far end of the hallway glowed pale yellow. At least one candle must still be burning on the lower floor. Her curiosity overcame her nervousness.

Descending halfway down the stairs into the warmth of the living room, at first she thought she was alone. The fire guttered on the grate. All the candles were out except the two on the table beneath the manuscript painting. They illuminated what she took to be a chair with a blanket or rug thrown over it. Only when he moved did she realize that it was David, dressed in some kind of dark robe with a hood, sitting cross-legged on the floor in front of the painting. He stood up, the hem of the robe swirling around his bare feet.

"He said you would come. He knew you were awake."

"David?"

"I was meditating. I lose track of time when I meditate. He takes control and I lose track of time."

She looked around the room. There was no one else. She tried to keep her voice from trembling.

"I guess I'll go back to bed."

"No, Eleanor, come down. We have things to talk about before the sacrament."

"David, are you drunk?"

84

"Not with wine."

He was seriously creeping her out. She fought the impulse to run back up the stairs and bolt her bedroom door. Instead, she descended to the living room.

"Come over here, I want you to hear his voice."

"David, you're making me nervous."

He laughed lightly and extended his hand. Hesitantly, she advanced toward him. There was something different about his face. At first she could not identify the strangeness in the shadow of the hood that covered his head, but then she realized that his eyes had changed color. They were no longer pale blue, but had become reddish-brown, the color of sooty amber.

"Are you wearing colored contact lenses?"

"Stand over here, where he can see you, and listen."

She forced herself to move toward him, and as she did so, he stepped back and gestured at the painting.

"Listen."

Something compelled her to turn her face to the painting on the wall. Once her eyes met those of the djinn, she found that she could not look away. There was such force in that glare of fury, but also deep, ancient wisdom. As she stared at his eyes, his lips writhed and twisted as though speaking, and she heard – something. It was not words, not even ideas in a formal sense, but what underlies these things.

He spoke to her in silent music and blind patterns. There was invitation in that unheard voice, seduction, the promise of wonderful gifts beyond anything she had ever dreamed. She might have rushed forward to embrace it, but beneath the promise there was something else, something that slithered in sticking mud and through stagnant pools of black water, over bleached white bones, across arid sands, beneath ancient trees from which dripped beards of poisonous moss. Time ceased to exist. Her world became no more than the silent hiss of his voice.

In the end, he released her. She could not have broken free from his hold over her mind had her life depended on it. She staggered back, and only then realized that she was still standing. Hands supported her, kept her from collapsing to the floor. His face was close to hers. Then he shrugged back the hood of his robe, and it became David's face.

"What's happening?" Her mind would not focus. In its background she still heard slithering silence.

"It's time for the sacrament. Rejoice, Eleanor. Out of all the women in this world, he has chosen you."

"You … planned this …?"

"He needed a pure vessel, a fertile vessel free from the contaminants of abortive prophylactics and pills, a vessel who would be ready to receive his sacrament at the time he chose to bestow it." A gleam of his normal self broke through the dancing shadows of madness in his strangely colored eyes. "Do you know how hard it is to find a virgin in Colorado who isn't on birth control?"

"How could you know … I was a virgin?"

"I talked to your friends. It took me months to ingratiate myself into their trust, but eventually they told me everything about you."

"Months?"

"The god and I have been planning this for a long time, ever since I accidentally burned through the pentacle John Dee had placed on the back of his image. That broke the binding spell, you see."

She rolled her eyes to the picture. "You freed him?"

"Not completely. But enough for him to enter my thoughts and speak to me, as he spoke to you. We are both his instruments, Eleanor. We are his chosen ones, and this night we begin the creation of a new world."

He pressed her backward, down onto the lambskin rug in front of the smoldering fire. She began to squirm and struggle, but she had no strength. The sibilance in her head made her weak. He forced his knee between her thighs and tore off his robe with one hand. She saw his erection in the fire glow. Its sleepy eye regarded her impassively and shed a single silver tear. She realized that she was screaming. It sounded distant in her own ears, as though she were hearing it from outside the house. The pitch of her screams mounted up and up and up. Impatiently, he pushed down the loose band of her pyjama bottoms. Then he was inside her, tearing at her flesh with white-hot thrusts of pain. His sweating face bobbed above her, up and down, up and down.

Something gleamed at the corner of her eye. Without thinking, she reached for it, turned it, and brought it in an arc against the side of the bobbing mask. The shattering of glass as the bottle broke was the first normal sound to reach her ears since gazing at the picture. David rolled heavily off her and out of her. Sitting up, she saw that her thighs were wet and red.

In a daze, she stood reeling before the fire, her blood dripping onto the white fur of the rug as she tugged up her pyjama bottoms. Her brain would not function. The hiss was still there, seducing her, beguiling her, promising secrets and wonders. It was driving her mad. Somehow she had to make it stop. She pulled herself toward the picture by holding onto the mantel of the fireplace for support. Semjaza leered down at her. He raised his left hand and extended it to her, revealing the lewdness of his erection.

Clenching shut her eyes, she grasped the ebony frame in both hands and tore it off the wall, then groped back to the fireplace with her eyes still closed and threw it onto the fire. The crackle of flames and the sharp crack of the glass as it shattered made her look. The vellum leaf curled out of its frame as it burned. Inside her mind there arose a mute screaming. She watched it burn until nothing remained but black charcoal and sooty shards of broken glass.

A groan drew her attention to David, who rolled his head back and forth on the rug and squinted up at her. Half his face was covered in blood, but once again his eyes were watery blue. For several minutes he said nothing. She stood there, incapable of speech or movement. Her mind had gone numb. When he rolled to the side and forced his way up on one knee, she felt no fear. He stared past her at the wall where the picture had hung, then looked at the fireplace.

"What have you done?" His voice rose in pitch. "What have you done?"

"I set you free," she murmured.

He knelt staring into the fireplace. An expression of horror twisted his features.

"You pathetic, stupid little slut, don't you know what you've done?"

"You're free now." She said it like a mantra.

He twisted his head at an unnatural angle to glare up at her, and spoke as though speaking to a child.

"I told you, Semjaza is a djinn."

"I don't understand."

"The djinn are made of fire."

As he uttered these words, the flames on the grate blazed up, roaring like a lion that leaps on its prey. They danced with different colors, and extended themselves out of the fireplace, a tongue from a gaping mouth. No, she corrected herself as the flames shaped themselves, not a tongue, a hand.

The gigantic hand of fire closed itself around David. She heard his screams even above its thunderous roar. The waves of heat beating against her skin made her step backward with her arms up to shield her face. For a moment she thought she too was burning.

David's body writhed in the grasp of the flaming fingers, then twitched and went still. The flames blackened him from toe to crown. The last of his hair burned away from his skull with a crackle. His body fell to the hearth rug as the flames withdrew themselves. What remained on the rug could not be recognized as human. It was drawn up upon itself, contorted into a knot of sooty bones and sinews. The skull grinned up at her from the floor.

"Is it over?" she whispered without realizing she had spoken.

As if in answer, the flame extended itself into the room, roaring like the wind of a hurricane. This time it was shaped into a head. She recognized the features of Semjaza as the head twisted on a neck of fire to glare at her. Its flaming lips curled back from its teeth. Two arms of flame emerged from the fireplace and began to push against the stones at its sides, forcing fiery shoulders out into the room one after the other.

The heat was unbearable. Each time she gasped for breath, it seared her lungs. She found herself unable to move. Like a rat hypnotized by the gaze of a snake, she could only watch as the gigantic body of the djinn emerged. The pine boards of floor in front of the fireplace began to burn, and the blood-stained lambskin rug smoldered and turned black. It was like watching the process of birth. When his legs slid free and he stood, he was forced to bow his head beneath the arched ceiling, the oak beams of which burst into flames.

Somehow, she did not know how, she found herself running through the snow. It was up to her knees and still falling thickly from the leaden sky. She reached her SUV and jerked open the rear door. Behind her, the windows of the chalet began to explode one by one. She did not dare to turn her head, but pulled out her skis. It took her only a minute to attach her ski boots to the bindings. She slid her feet into them and snapped the buckles shut. The boots felt loose, but that was because her feet were bare. Grabbing the ski poles, she paused to take one look over her shoulder.

The djinn stood in the midst of the burning chalet, his flaming head and shoulders projecting through a gap in the roof. As she watched, the rest of the roof fell in around him. He was larger than before, at least thirty feet tall. The fire seemed to nourish him. He stared at her and his voice whispered silently in the back of her mind.

"No!" she shrieked.

With a thrust of both ski poles, she sent herself flying over the new-fallen snow.

3.

The silence of the snow was broken only by the dull roar of the burning house. There was almost no wind until she began to gather speed down the slope of the road, and then it whistled in her ears and tore at the hem of her robe. Her mind was locked on only one thing – escape. She risked a glance over her shoulder.

A tall column of flame extended up from the burning roof, twisting a hundred feet into the slate-colored sky like the cone of a tornado. Working her poles to build speed, she glanced back again, and saw additional twists of flame branch from the main column like limbs. They defined a shape that was vaguely humanoid. The fiery form stepped out of the burning wreck of the house and took a stride down the road. Then it was hidden from sight behind a cluster of dark pines.

The slope of the winding road frustrated her. It was steep enough to keep her gliding over the soft powder, but not steep enough to allow her to gather any real speed. Her skis were made for downhill, not cross country. The snow was too soft and deep for her poles to be of much help. Behind her she heard a fluttering roar, like the sound of a burning log swung through the air. It was followed by a serpentine hiss of melting snow. The sounds were repeated, and repeated again, each time a little closer. Her heart turned to ice when she understood their meaning. The thing was following her on its legs of fire, stalking her across the snow. Around her crept an orange glow, but she did not dare look back again.

89

A cry of frustration escaped her lips. She was moving too slowly. The thing of fire gained on her with each great stride. There was only one way to go faster – she threw herself off the edge of the road and onto the steep shoulder of the mountain. There were boulders and trees in her path, but the glow of the sky was bright enough to show these obstructions. She had always been told that she was a good skier. Now she used every skill she had ever learned to stay on her feet. She was going faster than she had ever skied before in her life. She took no notice of the snowflakes stinging her eyes, the wind cutting at her bare fingers. The only thing that mattered was the need to keep moving, and not to fall. Behind her, the snow hissed at each gargantuan footfall of the djinn, but for the moment at least they did not draw closer.

She did not know where she was going until she got there – a small wooden house with two gasoline pumps in front of an attached garage. Above the garage was a sign: *Sam's Gas*. It was dark, but a tow truck stood beside the pumps. She pushed through the evergreen trees that bordered the road and crossed the road to the gas station. Mind numbed with terror, she pounded on the wooden door of the house, the ski pole still clenched in her fist. Words came babbling from her throat, but she had no awareness of what she said. She found herself screaming. Behind her on the road, the snow hissed.

A dim light flickered in the window beside the door, and the door jerked inward. An elderly man with a white beard and white hair stared wide-eyed into her face. He wore faded flannel pyjamas and held an oil lamp in one hand, a revolver in the other. She tried to push past him but he instinctively blocked her way.

"What's wrong? What's going on?" he demanded.

The cold light from the sky turned orange and red. The old man looked up and his mouth opened. She darted to the side and pushed off with her poles just before she heard the gun shots and the scream. Something exploded behind her with a wet bursting noise, like a liquid-filled bladder cast into a fire. She pushed herself into the road, then through the trees at its edge and once more down the side of the mountain. She was almost at its base, and it had begun to flatten out. An explosion from behind knocked the air from her lungs. Somehow she kept upright. It was followed a few seconds later by a second explosion. The sky lit up, and for a few seconds the roar of burning gasoline reached her ears. The roar faded behind, and once again she heard only the hiss of her skis.

She found herself praying.

"Please, Gracious Mother, let it linger in the burning house," she thought. "Let it linger, let it linger."

The dark pines opened into a large meadow. On its other side she saw the distant lights of windows. A town. She remembered driving through it on the way up. But it was too far away, much too far. She barely crawled through the drifts of snow, and once again behind she heard the roaring strides of the djinn as it stepped without haste out of the pines. The trees caught fire as it brushed them and framed the djinn like flaming torches. She dug hard in frustration with both poles, bending almost double at the waist, and the poles skidded out behind her, almost sending her sprawling across the snow.

It was then she knew that Semjaza, an ancient being of primordial evil whose existence she had not been aware of a few short hours ago, would catch her. She felt like an exhausted mouse, trapped in the middle of an open floor by a cat. She would be played with, tormented perhaps, and then what? Killed? Or did the djinn have some other intention? Surely its lust was satisfied. She remembered David's words and wondered why the djinn had selected her so carefully. Had it been just to rape her while possessing David? For that it could have used any woman.

She remembered that the Watchers had sired offspring on the Daughters of Men in the old biblical story. Had David impregnated her? If so, what did the djinn want? The terrible suspicion began to grow in her mind that the impregnation was not finished, that David had only been the fleshly part of it, that there was still the fiery substance of the djinn to place inside her. This thought took the strength from her limbs. She fell forward and lay a few moments in the drift before pushing herself up on one arm to look behind.

He came forward in all his flaming glory, gargantuan but strangely full of grace, the movements of his limbs a sensuous dance of fiery serpents in the near darkness. At the top of the whirling column of flame she could distinguish a face. Two eyes that were like burning stars stared from the orange and yellow flames. He stepped toward her, and the hiss of his foot pressed into the snow was so piercing, it made her clap her hands over her frozen ears. Another step, and another, until he towered above her and she felt the heat radiate from his body onto her bare skin. Slowly, with great care, he reached down one sinuous fiery arm.

There was a crack like a rifle shot, then a crash. A gout of white steam roared up from the snow. The sounds repeated themselves when the burning giant tried to take another step, and she saw on his fiery face something that looked like surprise, followed by an expression of dismay. The flaming columns of his legs began to sink into the snow, engulfed in white steam. It was as if the snow was eating the fire. Down he dropped until his waist was level with the drifts. The djinn cast a look of pure fury at her as he struggled to escape, but his efforts only caused him to sink more quickly.

Then she saw the water around his fiery chest, and understood. It was not a meadow she has skied into, but a frozen lake. The djinn extended his arm across the snow, striving to reach her with his fingers of fire. They brushed her legs, and she felt heat enter at her knees and fill her entire body, but his arm was not long enough to grasp her. With a hollow howl like distant wind between the rocks, the djinn's head sank beneath the surface, and then there was only a mountain of rising steam that gradually lessened as the water ceased to boil.

How long she lay there, she could not later have told. Her mind was empty, but strangely calm. The sounds of snowmobiles brought her back to her senses. The flames had been noticed by men from the town. They asked her what had happened, but she could not answer. They asked her if she was hurt. She realized then that she felt nothing. It was as if she had no body, only a still, quiet center of awareness in some distant safe place. She felt nothing at all, except ... yes, between her legs, a burning.

CRUISING

Tires shrieked on sun-baked asphalt, and the music of a car radio emptied itself across the quiet city intersection. Inside the car Johnny Sheen tapped his fingers impatiently on the steering wheel and looked up at the red light. He was bored. Aching for something to happen. It was a summer Sunday afternoon, and the streets of the city were like lanes through a graveyard.

Sheen was young and tough – what they call street smart. He had never read a book, but he knew what he wanted from life. His hair was razored in a spiky punk look and he wore mirror shades to hide his eyes. Drove a 78 Camaro with custom flame painted on the sides. The days he worked as a mechanic in a garage to earn enough for the upkeep on the car. Nights and weekends he cruised the streets. Cruising for action was his life.

An old Chevy sedan pulled up beside him in the fast lane. He gunned his engine and looked across with the faint mocking smile that never left his lips. Two teenage girls with long greasy hair and t-shirts sat in the front seat of the Chevy. His eyes measured the car professionally. Dented and covered with dust, it had come a long way. The windows were rolled down against the heat. He noticed a steel ring around the roof column, probably to keep the front door shut, and a line of ugly red decals on the front fender.

The brunette, who sat nearest him, looked over archly at the sound of his engine. Johnny smiled, knowing she could not read his eyes. She leaned over to the blonde driver and whispered into her ear, then glanced back at him. The blonde looked and laughed.

The light went green. He let them win and fell in behind, stalking them with animal patience. This was his game and he always came out on top in the end. They looked like sluts, but he was in no mood to be critical. Sunday afternoon was slow. He followed close and drafted them around a corner, the tires of both cars screaming. The brunette waved her hand at him through the dusty rear window, laughing, as the driver wove her way through the light traffic. Sheen stayed on her bumper, his interest growing. She might be a slut, but she drove like a bitch.

Another red. He swerved right and pulled close beside the Chevy, the music from his radio pacing his pulse beat. The faces of the girls were flushed with excitement, the driver's red mouth cruel as she raced her engine. Laughing wildly, her friend reached across through the open window of the Camaro and caressed Sheen's cheek. He took her finger into his mouth and bit it lightly, then leaned out of the car and met her lips with his in a bruising kiss that was broken abruptly as the blonde raced through the changing light.

Cursing, Sheen opened his four-barrel and went after them. The Chevy was a sleeper with dual pipes and big inches under the beaten metal, but the Camaro pulled even as the girls got held up in traffic. Waiting for an open stretch, he swung in close beside and reached through the window of the Chevy with both cars moving fast. Tauntingly the brunette let him touch her breast, then pulled away across the seat. The blonde cut the Chevy left and Sheen followed, his nerves tingling as his eyes flicked between the road ahead and the wicked faces beside him.

Once again he reached through the window of the other car. Something hard closed on his seeking arm. He looked across and saw a shining steel ring around his wrist, a short chain trailing from it to a similar ring around the roof column. The brunette held a key up by her face and shook it in front of him like a little bell. Leaning forward to watch, the driver smiled and trailed the tip of her tongue wetly over her lips.

It was a second before he understood. Then he felt a fear so naked that his stomach churned and his throat constricted and his skin went cold in the summer heat. He began to stop his car and hesitated, foot over the brake, realizing that he could not. As the Camaro slowed, the steel chain of the handcuffs pulled tight and sent a stab of pain lancing down his left arm. He carefully pressed the gas and matched speed with the Chevy.

The cruel smile left the face of the blonde driver and was replaced by calculation. The other watched him breathlessly. With deliberate skill the blonde swung the Chevy in slow curves from side to side, careful to let the Camaro keep pace. Sheen shouted and begged, forced to use every fraction of his skill to control the distance between the cars. His eyes flicked to the speedometer. Forty-five. The Chevy began to accelerate.

Ahead in the right lane was a slow-moving car that grew rapidly as they overtook it. Desperately Sheen swung into the Chevy, trying to force it wide to the left. Metal shrieked on metal as the doors ground against each other, but the old sedan was like a rock on the road. Pulling away, he tried to climb out his open window, almost lost the Camaro, and fought frantically to regain control. The girl with the key to the handcuffs leaned over and playfully bit one of his fingers.

Sheen never felt it. As the Chevy swerved to pass the slow car, drawing him tight against his door, time jammed like a single frame of film in a projector. He saw the looming rear of the slow car ahead; the excited, soulless faces watching him. For the first time he noticed that the line of decals under the road dust on the fender of the Chevy were tiny red hands broken off at the wrists and dripping blood.

Then time started up again and Johnny Sheen screamed.

FUTURE INDEFINITE

They were chanting in the street again below the open window. For a while they'd chant, and then they'd rest to recover their voices. It was a warm early evening on the second of September and the office of the *Hillbury Roundabout* was only two flights up.

"What do we want? Kill the pigs! When do we want it? Now!"

It was a chorus of hoarse, mostly female voices led by a bullhorn.

Ben Morton sighed and took off his paper thinking cap, which was shaped much the same as the paper sailor caps of young boys. Wearing the cap was an old habit. He used to believe it helped him write. Lately it didn't seem to be working. He rubbed his eyes in hope of making them focus on the computer screen.

"You could shut the window," Sal Meers suggested without looking up from her desk.

"Air conditioner's busted."

"When did that happen?"

"I don't know."

Her cynical gray eyes studied him.

"Go home, Morton. You look worn out."

"Can't. Got to finish this human interest piece."

"What's it about?"

"Man digging a garden in his back yard finds Civil War era tombstone inscribed with the name of an unknown soldier. When he tries to tell the authorities about it he gets arrested."

"Why did he get arrested?"

"I don't know. I guess it's illegal to have a Civil War tombstone."

She grunted.

"Leave your terminal on. I'll finish it for you."

He looked at her.

"You would do that?"

"Why not? I can churn out meaningless tripe by the ream. I've been doing it since there were people alive who knew what a ream is."

The *Roundabout* was a local newspaper distributed free in stores. It was really not much more than a collection of advertising flyers, but to masquerade as a newspaper it needed articles of local interest.

He rubbed the back of his neck and tried to raise his shoulders, but the muscles in his back started to cramp.

"Thanks."

His worn leather jacket hung from a hook of the antique wooden coat stand. Another hook supported his porkpie hat. He slid his arms through the sleeves of the jacket, which had long ago molded itself to the shape of his body, and snugged the back band of the hat down on his head.

Sal lit a cigarette and picked a flake of tobacco off the tip of her tongue with red fingernails.

"Why do you wear that ugly thing?"

"I like hats."

"Are you going bald, Morton? Men only wear hats when they're going bald."

"Good-bye, Sal."

She waved her cigarette at his back.

"Watch yourself. This crazy world swallows you up, and sometimes it doesn't spit you out."

The elevator was out of order, as it was most of the time. He ignored it and took the stairs. The building had been put up in the forties and showed its age. Tiles had fallen off the walls in the stairwell, The oak treads were worn in the center by decades of cheap shoes on tired feet.

A milling crush of humanity overflowed the sidewalk. The warm night had drawn them out of their stifling boxes to watch the demonstration. The protesters stood in the street, waving fists and screaming at the police precinct house on the other side. A line of cops in blue uniforms confronted them.

He wondered what they were protesting this time? Was it something the police had done, or something they had failed to do? The clash of angry voices hurt his ears.

A young woman with a shaved head grabbed him by the arm. Her heavily made-up face was streaked with tears. Black, wet smudges of mascara ringed her startling grey eyes.

"Are you Blue?" she shouted.

"What?"

"Are you with Blue Front?"

He bent his face closer to hers.

"Blue what?"

"We have to get out of here. It's going down any minute."

She tugged him fiercely along the sidewalk against the drift of the churning mob. He started to pull away, but the police came across the road in a blue wall with their riot shields raised, waving clubs and pepper spray. The casual spectators panicked and fled in all directions. He found himself in a stampede of sweating humanity. Behind him, over the bark of the police bullhorn, he heard something that sounded like a single gunshot.

Under the streetlight where they paused for breath, he saw that the woman was really not much more than a girl of college age. She was slight of body, almost elf-like. Even with the heels on her shoes raising her a couple of inches, she stood no higher than his chin. Her enormous eyes sparkled with delight as she laughed.

"We stuck the pigs tonight."

Another gang of young men and women fleeing the protest pushed into his back and propelled the two of them along the street like chips of wood in a stream.

"Come in here," she yelled, and pulled him into a dark doorway.

"Where are we?"

"We'll be safe in here."

He found himself in a coffee house illuminated only by dim red lamps on round tables and along the edge of a stage. The tables were covered with red-and-white check cloths. On the stage, a woman sat on a high stool hugging an acoustic guitar. Her long hair looked orange in the reddish light, and she wore an old-fashioned ankle-length dress that was tie-died. He stared at it in fascination – it must be decades since he'd seen a tie-dyed dress.

"First, we take Manhattan, then we take Berlin," the musician sang in a doleful voice that was not quite on key.

They passed between the tables. Most were occupied by couples or foursomes. A man with a ponytail and a ragged beard give the girl a clenched fist as she passed, and she returned the salute.

"He knows what just went down," she whispered in Morton's ear.

They took a table at the back of the room. The air was filled with drifting blue wraiths of smoke, and the smell of marijuana was strong enough almost to make him gag. When the Goth waitress drifted past, they ordered black coffee and sipped it as they listened to the singer, who now sang about a fighter trapped behind enemy lines and forced to disguise himself as one of the enemy to survive.

"What happened to your hair?" he said.

"What do you mean?"

He pointed at her head. "It's a simple question. Are you taking chemo?"

She laughed with sudden understanding.

"Hell, no. It's a statement, that's all."

"What kind of statement?"

"It says I'm not a toy. I walk my own road, you know?"

He forced a smile. "Do you go to the university?"

"Second year."

"Do you have an apartment nearby?"

"Maybe," she said, suddenly coy.

An athletic young black man sat abruptly at their table.

"Did it go down?" he asked, ignoring Morton.

"I heard the shot," she said.

"Righteous," he said, nodding his head. "Too bad a brother had to be sacrificed."

He wore a white wife-beater T-shirt and a heavy gold chain. Sweat stained the armholes of the shirt and ran down his sides in damp tracks. His hair was a close-cropped Afro.

"Who is this with you?"

"He's cool," the girl said. "The word went out for all men in Blue Front to wear hats."

He studied Morton up and down with amused disdain, his dark eyes settling on the wrinkled porkpie hat.

"I wouldn't get caught dead in that thing."

"I like old style," Morton told him.

"Shit. Whatever." Turning back to the girl, he said, "I'm going to see you tonight at the party, right?"

"I don't know, maybe."

He stood up and leaned down to point his finger at her.

"I'm going to see you tonight."

"Who was that?" Morton asked as the black man worked his way between the tables.

"Hassan. We hang sometimes."

"Is he one of us?"

She nodded. "He works the streets. You know, the knock-out game. Last week he put an old Jew in the hospital."

"That's part of it?"

"Didn't you know?"

He shook his head.

"We have to instil fear into the hearts of the prols, right? Make them afraid to come out of their little houses."

"I guess we do."

"He's all right. He tried to volunteer for tonight, but the organizers had someone already picked."

"Too bad. Maybe he'll get his chance next time."

"Yeah, maybe." She look at him curiously, making him wonder if he'd said the wrong thing.

"We should get back to my place, if we're going. I've got early classes tomorrow."

"Sounds like a plan."

They left the coffeehouse and continued down the street. The night began to boom with a Latino beat. A vintage dark sedan pulled up beside them with all its windows cranked down. There were four men in the car.

"Hey, Cherry," the driver said. "You need anything?"

The girl thought about it as she walked. "Guess so. What you got, Salt?"

"We got nothing but we're going to get something now. Why don't you and your date come with us? We'll treat you right."

"We should just go to your place," Morton said.

She hesitated and frowned.

"No, I want something tonight. I'm so hyped up, you know?"

The back door of the sedan opened and one man got out. Morton and the girl crawled into the back seat and found themselves squeezed between two Puerto Ricans, or so Morton judged them to be by their accents. The car and its crew alike reeked of marijuana and stale beer. Latino noise spilled from the radio as the car lurched from the curb.

"How far is it?" Morton asked, raising his voice to make himself heard. There was no response. He repeated the question.

"Not far, Mr. Citizen. You be cool, alright?" the driver said, meeting Morton's eyes in the mirror. They shifted to the girl.

"You hear what went down tonight, Cherry?"

The girl glanced at Morton and shook her shaved head.

"No. What went down?"

"The cops iced a black dude during the protest."

"Holy shit," she said.

He laughed and nodded.

"The pigs can't claim they were just doing their job this time. The news on the radio says they shot him in the back."

The further they drove, the darker and quieter the streets became. Many of the street lights were smashed out and had not been replaced. There were stripped hulks of cars by the curb, old sofas with their seat cushions torn open, and piles of garbage spilling out of their bags. A black cat ran through their headlight beams as the car slowed.

"There he is," one of the Puerto Ricans said.

Salt turned off the radio and slowly pulled into an unpaved parking lot behind a boarded-up store. The lot was empty except for a single pickup truck with a fibreglass cap on the back. The sedan idled up parallel to the truck, but facing the other direction.

"You open for business?" Salt asked the driver, who leaned out of his open window and studied their faces.

He was a young redneck with ragged blonde hair and a fistful of freckles scattered across the bridge of his broken nose. The man in the other side of the truck might have been his younger brother. He was thinner, smaller.

"What you need?" the redneck said past the toothpick in the corner of his mouth.

"What have you got?" Salt asked.

"Come back to my store and I'll show you."

Everyone got out. Morton's legs were cramped from being folded up for so long. He followed the others to the back of the truck, and the redneck dropped the tailgate. A light came on. He pulled a metal box from under a coil of rope and opened it, then began taking out small plastic vials of pills. His brother stood a little distance away with his arms crossed on the denim vest he wore.

"You got any coke?" Salt asked.

"Yeah, I got coke." The redneck dug in the box and brought out another vial. He held it up and shook the white powder in it. "How much you need?"

Salt took a gun from the back of his pants and pointed it.

"I guess I'll take it all, John Boy."

Everything happened fast. The younger redneck went for his gun. Salt shot him once in the face and one of the other Puerto Ricans shot his brother three times in the chest. Salt stuffed the vials back into the metal box, slammed it shut and put it under his arm.

"Let's get the fuck out of here."

The big sedan scattered dirt and gravel as its spinning rear wheels grabbed the asphalt on the street. The Puerto Ricans started to laugh.

"We got enough here to spend the winter in Florida," Salt said.

"You're such a bastard," Cherry told him. "You know I can't get involved with the police."

"Relax, chica, you didn't do nothing."

"That's not how the law works, Salt."

"What's done is done."

She did not argue, but she glared at Morton and shook her head, mouthing the word "asshole."

They drove in a long loop through the dark city. The neighborhoods began to improve. The streets widened and the old cars and garbage disappeared. They passed the wrought-iron gates of a manor house on a low hill. Through the wrought-iron pickets of the fence, cars were moving around the circle of the crush gravel drive, stopping to emit well-dressed couples. The cars that were not chauffeured were driven away by valets.

"Stop here," Cherry said.

The dark sedan coasted to the curb. Salt surveyed the line of cars through the fence. "You sure you got the right house?"

"I know the people who live here."

He lifted the metal box, which rested in his lap, and rattled its contents. "Want some of this?"

"No. Just let us out."

They watched the sedan slide quietly away. The sound of classical music reached them from the open front doors of the house on the hill.

"I think I better leave you here," Morton said.

"Don't be silly. These people are my friends. We can get something to eat, maybe find an empty room to crash."

He allowed himself to be led up the drive and into the bright lights that bathed the stately facade of the house. No one gave them any attention, not even the husky menservants who stood on either side of the front door.

Morton realized he was woefully underdressed for the occasion. All the men wore dark suits or tuxedos, and the women were adorned in brightly colored gowns. There were a few young men in pullover sweaters and blazers, but even their more casual clothing screamed quality.

"If anyone asks, you're my guest," Cherry said, holding his arm in hers.

The gathering was made up of older men and younger women. There were a few exceptions – mature women fighting the good fight against time with the aid of plastic surgery and expert makeup, hanging on the arms of vivacious young men who exuded charm. They were the kind of men it was impossible to dislike, even if you tried to do so. Diamonds on bare throats and earlobes and fingers glittered and flashed.

Cherry vanished with the first minute inside the house. Morton found himself being witty to strangers and drinking Chablis. Unless it was just the wine that made him think he was being witty. Anyway, no one complained and he wasn't thrown out.

The conversation ranged over the social and political topics of the day. Most of the opinions were what Morton liked to think of as conservative liberal. They were liberal, but not radical enough to raise an eyebrow.

"Did you hear about the shooting of the African American at the protest earlier tonight?"

He blinked to focus his eyes on the tall woman with black hair cut in a pageboy style who stood before him. Everything about her was elongated – her neck, her face, her nose, her fingers, which were stained yellow with tobacco. Her bloodshot eyes stared at him with a complete lack of emotion. It was like looking at the face of a grotesque doll.

"Terrible thing, just tragic," he murmured, looking around for Cherry.

"Eat me," a woman said.

He turned and saw a petite blonde in a maid's uniform with a silver tray. The tray was filled with small chocolate rosebuds.

"What's in them?"

She touched her finger to her lips. "I'm sworn never to tell."

"I'll pass."

"Maybe later?"

"Doubtful," he said, and watched her walk across the floor between the milling groups engaged in animated chatter.

His empty glass was taken and another pressed into his hand. The floor was beginning to turn under his feet in a pleasant and perfectly controllable manner. He felt the urge to do a dance step to show how in control he was, but decided to save it for the right moment.

"The old man wants to examine you."

There was Cherry, standing in front of him.

"What old man? The old man of the sea?"

She pursed her full lips and shook her head in mock disapproval.

"Baby shouldn't have eaten the rosebuds."

"But I didn't eat the rosebuds."

He found himself drawn along through a choppy froth of humanity, surrounded by loud conversation punctuated by irregular bursts of laughter. Some of the eyes rolled and followed him as he passed with a poorly drawn paper smile taped in place on his face.

They drifted into a room where two naked women were having sex on a large table. People gathered around to watch stood and sat in varying stages of undress, mouths joined, hands pressed between legs.

The girl would not let him pause to watch. She pulled him impatiently through a room that had a revolving mirror ball on the ceiling – or it may have been a crystal chandelier, Morton was not sure which. Everyone was dressed in furry animal costumes that completely covered their heads and bodies. Most couples were fucking from the rear after the manner of horses, cows, and donkeys. A cow mooed loudly with her horned head thrown back as she rode a grizzle bear that lounged on its back in a leather armchair. From somewhere in the room the children's song "Down on Animal Farm" played loudly.

He entered a space without walls where the light was too bright and composed of electric blue and bright orange and a kind of chartreuse. Creatures that looked like elongated numerals were dancing with each other. Suddenly a flood of pink tetrahedrons rained down from the ceiling and all the dancing figures fell to their knees and competed with each other to pick them up in their mouths.

"Come in, sir, come in."

He blinked and realized he stood in the doorway of an old-fashioned library. Cherry gave him an encouraging smile and shoved him into the room, then closed the sliding panel doors behind him. The doors cut out most of the sounds from the party.

An older man with white hair and a white goatee beard and whiskers, who looked a little bit too much like Colonel Sanders, came forward from the fireplace and escorted him to a wing-backed chair covered in button-tufted green leather. The old man sat in a similar chair and regarded Morton as he smoked a cigar. Morton relaxed and felt the heat of the leather against his back. There was a fire burning in the fireplace, and the room was a little warmer than necessary in spite of the air conditioning.

"I've been impressed by what you've written over the past year, very impressed," the old man said.

As he spoke, a line of sparks floated out of the fireplace and made a kind of crown or halo as they slowly circled his head.

Morton thought back on his recent articles for the *Hillbury Roundabout*. One was about a boy crippled in a fall from a horse who was learning to walk with the aid of crutches. Another concerned the second marriage of an elderly couple on their eightieth anniversary. And he had also written a piece on the rising incidence of dog bites in the public park.

"Sir, I believe you have me confused with somebody else."

"There's no confusion, Mr. Morton."

Hearing his name from the lips of a complete stranger focused his mind to a surprising degree. The crown of sparks vanished from about the head of the old man.

"You have me at a disadvantage."

"My name is Barnard Jamison."

The name sounded familiar.

"Senator Jamison?"

"I'm retired now, son. I got tired of politics and decided to take up a new occupation."

"What would that be?"

"Insurrection. I head a covert circle of anarchists sometimes known as Blue Front."

Morton felt suddenly cold over all of his body.

"That shooting of the black man tonight?"

"Part of a program of social destabilization. Unfortunate, but sacrifices must be made in war, and make no mistake about it, we are at war."

"Look, Barnard, you shouldn't be telling me this. I'm not the man you think I am."

"You are Benjamin Morton, are you not?"

"Sure, but I'm just a hack writer for an advertising flyer that masquerades as a newspaper."

"You publish your work on the Internet under the pseudonym Nomad, is that right?"

Morton stared at the old man, who still made him think of fried chicken. There was no way Jamison could possibly know about his Internet alias. He had taken pains to conceal his trail and had constructed a false identity for Nomad.

"I don't know what you're talking about."

The old man laughed until his belly shook.

"I'm talking about the set of articles you wrote for the international anarchist site Red April. Certain people were very impressed by them. It's the reason you are here talking to me."

"I'm here because a ditzy girl thought I was somebody else."

"There are no accidents in my line of work, son. You are here because I want you here."

"What do you want from me?"

"Let's talk first about the state of the nation. What do you think of it?"

"I think it stinks."

He chuckled.

"So do I, son, so do I. People can't find work that pays enough to live on. The food and the water make us sick. Racial hatred threatens to rip the country apart at the seams. Violent crime makes the cities unliveable. The schools can't teach and the children can't learn. Politicians do nothing but lie as they take bribes from the wealthy. Illegals pour across the southern border. Gun violence is on the rise. The family unit is falling apart. Pornography, drug addiction, and welfare have destroyed our culture. What do you say to that?"

"I'd say that's about right."

"What would you say if I told you that we caused it all?"

I looked at him with incomprehension.

"All what?"

"All the problems I named, and a lot more besides. What would you say if I told you that our organization was the root cause of all the problems that plague society?"

"If I believed you, I guess I'd ask why you did it."

He puffed on his cigar, looked at the ceiling and blew smoke upward, then regarded me with ancient, cynical eyes.

"You can't build something without destroying something else, isn't that right?"

I thought about it. "I guess that's right."

"Well, we're building a new America. We can't build it until we remove the old America that stands in its way. If you want to put up a new school on the same land where an old school stands, you first have to tear down the old school. We're charged with the task of tearing down the old America and throwing its pieces into the trash. Once we clear away the rubble, others will begin to build the new America, an America that will fit into the plan of the New World Order that is being enacted all around the globe even as we sit here, talking to each other."

"I understand what you're saying but I don't understand what my part will be."

"Your persuasive skills as a writer are crucial at this juncture in the deconstruction process to insure that the general population remains placid and undirected. It will be your task to keep the people divided along racial lines and by petty social issues such as abortion and homosexual marriage. You will attack any bastion of the old culture that offers hope or can be used as a rallying point around which a resistance could begin to form itself."

"I doubt if the editor of the *Hillbury Roundabout* will go for it," I said with a smile, wondering if he was serious or insane.

Jamison waved his cigar.

"That's all over and done with. From now on you'll write for the best newspapers and news magazines in the world. Everything you write will be published. You'll win writing awards. You'll become a celebrated media spokesperson. You'll write books and they will become bestsellers."

"You paint a rosy picture. And in return, all I have to do is write what you tell me to write."

"No, you write what you've already been writing on Red April. We'll see that it gets noticed in the right places. You don't have to change your views for us, son. You're already one of us. You just didn't know it."

I sat back and thought about all that money, all that fame. The awards, the bestsellers, the celebrity. I won't say I wasn't tempted.

"I'm not one of you, Jamison."

He frowned. "Don't be a fool, Morton. Think what you stand to gain."

I reached into my pocket and turned off my audio recorder, then took the little custom-made .32 automatic from its hiding place and shot him once through the forehead. It was a tiny thing with a built-in silencer and the bullets were subsonic. It barely made a pop.

The doors of the library opened.

"Has Daddy convinced you to join us yet?" Cherry asked as she turned and shut the doors behind her.

I waited for her to face me. To her credit, she did not scream when she

109

saw her father on the floor. Her expression of confusion quickly became one of calculation.

"I need to know a few things," I told her.

"Shoot," she said, and giggled.

"You didn't mistake me for one of your father's agents just because I wear a hat?"

"No, I knew who you were."

"Those four Puerto Ricans. They didn't just happen along, did they?"

"They were supposed to drive us directly to this house. I didn't know they had a drug buy planned."

"One more thing. That black guy who got shot in the back by a Blue Front agent, he was one of your own people, right?"

She nodded.

"Like the man said, sacrifices must be made."

I shot her through the heart. An expression of contempt stole across her pretty face as her body crumpled in upon itself. She ended up face down on the carpet.

A New World Order was coming, of that there was no doubt, but it remained undetermined what form that new order would take. I thought about the year I'd spent slaving away at the *Hillbury Roundabout*, waiting to be contacted by Blue Front, and wondered if it had all been worth it.

I had to believe that my side was the side of justice and reason. If I ever stopped believing that, I would lose all hope. My work tonight wouldn't end the cultural cold war that raged across the globe, but it removed one of the key pieces on the side of chaos from the game board. As small as that achievement was, it would have to satisfy me, at least for now.

WHAT IS HAPPENING

Elonzo Albergini awoke as he usually did, lying in the center of his enormous round bed, covered in a black silk sheet, with Mozart playing softly over the house sound system. The antique French clock beside the bed told him it was one in the afternoon, his usual hour for waking, but something was wrong, something was not as it should be, something was other than the way he had ordered it.

He slid the sheet down and looked at his enormous expanse of chest and the two elongated bags of skin and fat that were his breasts, and saw little bumps on his pale, hairless skin. Goosebumps. He was shivering because the air in his bedroom was cold instead of its usual 22 degrees Centigrade.

For a few moments he simply lay there, enjoying the novel sensation of being chilled. The embroidered curtain at one of his full-length windows billowed inward, and he saw through the gap exposed behind it that the pane of glass was broken – not just cracked but actually shattered. He lifted his head with difficulty on his corpulent neck and noticed pieces of glass over the highly polished hardwood floor. Amid the glass lay a pine bough, its white end ragged where it had torn away from its tree.

The curtain billowed again, and he saw a fresh layer of snow on his patio, and beyond that, white-capped mountains against a blue sky.

"Melita, where are you?" he yelled with some annoyance. "Come here, woman, and bring the pan. I need to take a piss."

It was not like his personal nurse to be absent when he woke. The staff of the house knew his habits. They all knew he woke at one. When the woman came he would demand an explanation. He wasn't paying her ten percent above the going rate for nothing.

Thinking about the fullness of his bladder made the pressure seem greater. Where was that infernal woman?

"Carlos, are you there? Find Melita and bring the bitch to me."

There was no answer from the rest of the house. The bedroom door was open, as usual, but it was possible his manservant Carlos had not heard him. He reached for his cell phone on the table beside the bed. It was always placed were he could reach it without straining when he woke. His range of movement was quite limited. He pressed the button that rang Carlos. The servant's phone rang but was not answered.

Elonzo cursed out loud. This was really too much to bear. He paid these people to be there when he needed them. They were a necessary part of his life. He could no longer rise from his bed due to his vast bulk. They had become his legs and arms, bringing him what he needed when he needed it, feeding him, bathing him, taking care of his toilet requirements.

This last thought made the pressure of his bladder increase yet again.

"Is anyone there? Anyone?" he shouted. "Marie? Samuel? Carlos? Melita?"

He lay listening to the silence. The curtain fluttered in the chill breeze that blew through the broken window, making him shiver again as he looked at it. This time there was no pleasure in the novelty.

Some household event must have disrupted the normally smooth procedures of his staff. Had last night's windstorm done more damage than just his broken window? If so he would have it repaired at once. He liked his house to be meticulous both inside and out.

He let out a noisy gust of irritation that should have sent someone running to him to timidly ask what was wrong, but there was nobody to hear it. Reaching for the remote control, he clicked on the wall-mounted television opposite the foot of his bed.

A woman's face appeared. There was soot on her cheeks and black channels of soot below her terrified eyes and flaring nostrils. She looked like a character in a horror movie. Behind her there was only a bare wall. She hugged a hand microphone close to her lips. The microphone picked up background noises that sounded like screams and explosions.

"Everyone should go to their designated emergency center immediately," she said in a voice distorted by shock. "We don't know if there will be a second wave of attacks but for your safety you must go to your emergency center. We will keep you updated as events unfold –"

The picture cut abruptly to background static, then to a blue screen. Elonzo grunted with displeasure. He didn't like these television dramas that pretended to be news broadcasts. He switched the channel, but it was blue as well. With his thumb he clicked through his favorite channels. All of them were off the air. As he was doing this, the electricity in the house failed. The only sounds were the burble of the little marble fountain in the corner of the room, and the flutter of the curtain.

He lay listening to the water. It was normally a soothing sound. That was why he had installed the fountain. Presently it only reminded him of his bladder. He wondered why it had not stopped running, then remembered that it functioned on water pressure, not electricity.

All of his anger had trickled away, replaced by a growing concern. He decided to call his private doctor and ask him what was going on. Doctor Malbu could come over to the house and take care of him until whatever had caused this disruption was sorted out.

The cell phone would not connect. The network must be down, knocked out by whatever had caused the power failure.

He tried to roll over on his side, but it was impossible. He was too heavy. He remembered the last time he had been able to roll over without help had been almost a year ago. Since then he had gained another thirty kilos, by Malbu's estimate – no one had actually weighed him in over a decade. He was just too big for ordinary scales, and in any case could not stand up on his own.

"Melita? Carlos? Anyone who can hear me, come here at once."

In the silence there came a vibration that shook the house. It was like an earthquake, only briefer. The windows rattled in their frames but no more of them broke. He lay listening in alarm. After almost a minute he heard a rumble, like distant thunder. He stared at the fluttering curtain but the glimpses it offered of the snow-covered patio and the far-off mountains contained no revelation.

A little more than an hour after the shaking of the house, his bladder gave way and emptied warm urine between his fat thighs, soaking the black silk sheet under him and the mattress beneath it.

He drew the top sheet up over his shoulders and put his teeth together to stop them from clattering. He could not remember a time when he had been so cold for so long. Even in childhood his life had been pampered, his every need cared for.

Periodically, he shouted the names of his household staff. Night fell without a response. He slept for a time. When he awoke again, it was to the cold and the damp and the smell of his own shit. During the night his bowels had released themselves beneath him.

The bubble of the fountain was maddening. His mouth was by this time as dry as cotton, so that when he tried to swallow he almost gagged on the dryness. He wondered why the fountain did not freeze, then reasoned that it was not cold enough. The air inside the bedroom was very close to freezing, but not below. He could see through the blowing curtain that the morning sun was melting the snow outside.

Every few hours he tried the television remote but the electricity never came back on. In the afternoon he made a valiant effort to get out of the bed, using all the strength in the atrophied muscles of his legs and arms. He succeeded is sliding half off the bed to the floor with the upper portion of the black sheet wrapped around his folds of fat like a shroud. The full-length mirror on the other side of the room give him a good look at himself as he lay on the floor, one flabby leg still on the bed, its foot tangled in the sheet.

He always slept naked. His skin looked pale and vulnerable in the glass. His fat head on his bloated neck would have resembled that of a newborn baby except for the coal-black hair that covered its scalp. He was proud of his hair. Baldness was not a part of his family's genetic heritage. He noticed with a pang of concern that it was wildly disordered, and that a day's growth of beard stubble covered his cheeks and neck. There was no one to comb his hair or shave his face. No one to feed him. No one to give him water.

Toward the end of the day he managed to work his foot free from the twisted sheet and rolled with great difficulty onto his stomach. It was hard to breathe with the weight of his obese body pressing down on his lungs. His fat spread out over the floor, concealing in its trembling mass the contours of his limbs.

He began to pull himself toward the bubbling marble fountain. By using the full strength of his arms and legs, he was just able to move his bulk a few inches at a time. After a few such lurching progressions, which resembled those of a sea lion, he had to rest to regain his strength. He could feel that strength beginning to fail from the cold, the hunger and the thirst.

At some point during the darkness of night he slept. When he woke on the third day, he began again. The muscles in his arms and legs shook with fatigue and cramped, so that he had to wait for long periods before he could attempt to use them. Even so, he did not give up. Whatever anyone said of Elonzo Albergini, no one ever suggested that he lacked determination.

He had no friends and many enemies. His business partners respected him, but it was respect born from fear. They knew how implacable he was in punishing anyone who crossed his purposes. He knew that all his servants hated him, but he paid them well enough to put their personal feelings aside. He trusted no one, confided in no one, loved no one.

Some men had a passion for women, others for violence, but his passion had always been food. Even as a young child he had been morbidly obese. His weight had never ceased to increase throughout his entire lifespan. He had established himself in business while still able to walk on his own legs without supports. After that, it didn't matter if he could walk. His wealth enabled him to hire others to care for all his needs.

Another night passed before he reached the fountain. It was a substantial structure of carved Italian marble. The pool lay in the base of a large bowl, the water level some distance below the rim. The stream of the fountain erupted out of an urn upheld on the shoulder of a naked boy and arched into the middle of the pool, which was about a meter from the rim.

Elonzo put one hand over the rim of the bowl but was not able to reach down into it far enough to touch the water. The rim was too high. He needed to get his elbow up to the rim so that he could reach downward on the other side. For several hours he tried to raise his bloated torso high enough, but failed. He could feel his strength slipping away. He was so cold. The chill had gone below his skin, below even the dense layers of fat, and buried itself in his muscles and bones.

Blood seeped from his cracked lips. He licked it, thankful for even this salty moisture. His tongue had swollen and was as dry as an old sock. The side of the fountain felt cold where it pressed against his cheek. He grunted and tried with all his strength to raise himself, then collapsed onto the floor, sobbing like a small child.

After a while, he managed to use the side of the fountain to roll onto his back, with his head and shoulders propped up against the marble. In front of him was the familiar shape of his bed, and beyond its foot the broken window where the curtain continued at intervals to balloon inward, giving him flashes of the world outside.

He stopped crying and started to laugh. It was some time before he could stop.

"So this is how it ends?" he said aloud, closing his eyes, his voice cracked with dryness. "God, I have never prayed to you before, but hear my prayer. I beg of you, in your infinite mercy, don't let me die alone."

The tinkle of a shard of glass and a low growl made him open his eyes. A wolf stood halfway through the broken window, watching him, lips curling away from its yellow fangs as it snarled. It advanced into the bedroom on stiff legs, all its senses alert. Elonzo shouted at it in his weakened voice. It danced backward, then after a few seconds resumed its slow advance. He saw that its sides were thin, its ribs clearly visible.

He kept shouting and waving his arms until these things had no effect on the wolf. It bit him on the foot and jumped away. Red blood welled out of the wound and pooled on the hardwood around his heel. He began to scream like an animal. It was a shrill noise, not something usually heard from a human throat. The wolf bit him on the calf while he was still screaming and shook its head back and forth, tearing out a chunk of soft, pink skin and fat with some trailing muscle tissue.

Behind the wolf Elonzo saw three wolf cubs enter through the broken window. For the first time he realized it was a female. The cubs were thin. They approached with snarling muzzles, each a miniature likeness of its mother.

"Why is this happening to me?" he demanded. "I don't understand."

The she-wolf leapt forward and tore out his fat throat. The grotesque bulk of his body rippled and lay still. Burbling noises from the rent in his throat mingled for a brief while with the cheerful bubbling of the fountain.

Licking the blood from her lips, the she-wolf stood on her hind legs with her forelegs on the rim of the fountain and leaned her head down to lap the cool water with her tongue.

THE SEED OF VASS

1.

A woman neither young nor old left the ruts in the frozen coach road and set her foot on a path that faded into shadows beneath the trees. She clutched her gray cloak tighter around her throat and glanced back the way she had come. Smoke from the chimneys of Salem Village hung like a shroud above the skeletal boughs of a copse of leafless oaks, but the village itself was hidden behind a rise. Lowering her head, she set off along the path with a determined stride.

Her stylish shoes with their silver buckles and silk bows were not made for such work. Puffs of white breath emerged from between her lips and hung under the broad brim of her hat on the still autumn air as she labored up slopes of dead leaves and browning grass, and over moss-encrusted fallen logs. The sky above her was a blue vault, but the golden sun shining through the trees low in the west gave no warmth.

She smelled wood smoke as she traced the faint path between ancient pillars strangely twisted by lightning and wind. A cabin emerged suddenly through a screen of willows. It was a low thing made from notched logs chinked with moss and mud. The roof was sod, the chimney of unmortared stones. The solitary window that faced her was shuttered. Gripped by sudden nervousness, she crept across the clearing on a rustle of frosty grass and hesitated at the door.

"Come in," a cracked voice called from the other side. "I've been expecting ye."

Gathering the remaining tatters of her courage, she lifted the wooden latch and pulled the door open.

"Shut it up, shut it up, you're letting in the cold."

An old woman sat on a stool before the fireplace wrapped in a filthy brown blanket. Tangled gray hair escaping from under a white cap framed her withered features and wild gray eyes. The younger woman wrinkled her nose. The cabin was filled with smells, none of them pleasant. Rotting meat, urine, sour sweat were among them. She reluctantly pulled the door in behind her. Some light found its way through the cracks in the window shutters, but most came from the red glow of the fire.

She saw the old woman's fingers moving in the dimness, and realized that she was braiding a cord. Along its length hung bent nails of black iron.

"Come over here where I can see ye."

She inched around the chair and stood beside the fireplace, grateful for the warmth its stones radiated against her thigh.

"Take off your hat so I can get a look."

Her face was thin but comely, her eyes a soft sea-green. The red in her long auburn hair was heightened by the firelight, and cold air had put a touch of color in her cheeks. That she was pretty was undeniable, yet there was a hardness in the faint lines at the corners of her mouth and eyes.

"Mother Wilde, I've come to ask ye –"

"What be your name, child?"

She hesitated. The old woman stared at her, waiting.

"They call me Moll Corey."

"Show me what you wear. Open it, open it."

Moll reluctantly parted her cloak to reveal her fiery red dress.

"So that's your trade," the old woman said, nodding. "I thought as much. Well, we all must eat. What be ye wanting of me?"

"They say in the town that ye make potions."

"Aye, that be true. What kind of potion would ye be needing? A love potion? Nay, your kind knows nothing of love."

The harlot licked her pale lips. "Do you swear what I say will be taken to your grave?"

Mother Wilde's laughter was like a rusty saw blade biting into hardwood.

"Who would dig me a grave? Like as not the wolves will feast on my flesh and crack my bones for marrow."

"Swear, or I cannot tell ye."

"Would you have me swear on a Bible?" The old woman turned her head with exaggerated care from side to side. "Do you see a Bible about?"

Moll bit her lower lip, then started toward the door.

"Stop this foolishness, child, and say what thou needs. It will go no further."

"A man, a gentleman he is, has done me a wrong."

"Jilted by your lover, were ye? You're not the first."

"I want him to suffer, and then I want him to –" She hesitated.

"You want old Mother Wilde to sell ye poison," the old woman said, nodding her head. "Say it."

"Yes," Moll said sharply. "I want him dead."

The old woman pursed her wrinkled lips and smiled, then shook her head.

"I won't sell ye poison to kill a man. Sheriff Corwin would be on me like a terrier on a rat."

"Sheriff Corwin and I have an arrangement. I will tell him not to trouble ye."

"Nay, girl, that's not good enough."

"Then I came all this way for nothing," Moll said in disgust.

"Now, now, be not so hasty, my young harlot. There be many ways to punish a man without killing him."

"How do ye mean?"

"Suppose I could make a potion that would cause your man to go about on all fours rooting in the dung heaps for food. With that satisfy your vengeance?"

Moll thought about it. She was reluctant to part with her determination to murder her former lover, but the picture painted by the old woman was attractive.

"Would he ever recover his senses?"

"Not likely. It addles the brain, ye see. He'd never be right again."

"How much would such a potion cost?"

"Nine silver shillings, not a penny more nor less."

"That is a large sum."

Mother Wilde eyed her up and down. "For a comely young lass such as yourself? Ye can earn it in a week."

Moll made up her mind. "When may I have it?"

The old woman looked into the fire. "I need to prepare some herbs. Come back in three days and I'll have it for ye. Bring the silver."

2.

In the afternoon of the third day Moll returned to the cottage in the wood. As before, the window was shuttered and the door shut. She went inside and stopped in surprise. Mother Wilde stood in the middle of the open floor, naked. Her thin limbs and sagging breasts gleamed in the firelight, both appalling and fascinating. She took milky salve on her fingers from a small stone jar and rubbed it on the insides of her thighs and through the gray tangle of pubic hair. She glanced at Moll and grunted.

"I've come for the potion," Moll told her.

"Not ready yet. Come back tomorrow."

"I have the money."

"Tomorrow, I tell ye. Today I have things to do and places to be."

Moll started to leave, but her curiosity won out over her revulsion. "What be ye doing?"

The old scarecrow cackled. "Have ye never heard of the flying ointment?"

The younger woman shook her head.

"We spread it on our skin, and it carries us away to distant lands."

This sparked a memory in Moll.

"I heard a story once of a witch who spread ointment over her limbs and fell into a swoon. When she waked she swore she'd been flying."

Mother Wilde made a sound of disgust and spat on the hard-packed dirt floor. "Such fools don't know the true ointment. They slurry their wits with henbane and nightshade. There's not many that knows how to make the real thing, for what goes into it comes not of this world."

"But if it can only be got from another world, how did ye make the first pot of ointment?"

The old woman frowned and grabbed her by the arm. Her clutching claw was surprisingly strong. She hustled the younger woman out the doorway.

"Tomorrow," she said, and slammed the door.

Moll walked away from the cabin, anger building inside her. To come so long a way on foot for nothing, and then to be treated like some guttersnipe by a crone who had lost her wits. She stopped at the edge of the clearing, fuming silently. Her temper was up. She decided to return and tell the old witch what she thought of her. Stalking back the way she had come, she threw open the door, her green eyes flashing with reflected firelight.

The cabin was empty. Moll stood with her hand on the latch and her mouth gaping as she stared around. It was a single room and it had no back door, but the old woman had vanished. She went in cautiously, fear thrilling along her nerves.

"Mother Wilde?"

A faint familiar cackle came as though from a great distance, but it seemed to be all around her and she could not guess its direction. She cocked her head, listening. The air hung heavy with the lingering scent of the ointment. A burning log broke in two on the hearth and sent up a shower of sparks, making her flinch. Her heart began to beat rapidly.

When nothing else happened, she gathered her wits and wandered around the cabin, looking for things to steal. To her disgust, she saw that the old woman owned nothing of value. Even her dishes and spoons were made of wood. The single exception was the stone pot of ointment. She picked it up. There was a strange carving on its lid, a kind of face that was not quite human, but neither was it any animal she knew. Twisting open the tight-fitting lid, she sniffed its contents, wrinkled her freckled nose at the pungent odor, then reclosed it and slid it into a pocket of her dress.

Shadows of twilight had fallen and the sky had turned the color of beaten lead when she emerged from the cabin. She walked quickly along the path with a sense that something followed her, but when she turned to look there was nothing. Even so, she felt eyes watching her from a dense growth of willows at the side, and once she heard a rustling in the dead leaves, but she told herself it was only a hare. Darkness gathered quickly, so that by the time she emerged onto the coach road the brighter stars were gleaming in a purple sky. A rising moon near its fullness lit her way back into Salem Village.

She went swiftly up the external stair to her room above Ingersoll's Ordinary and latched the door behind her, then stood listening for footfalls on the landing outside. The sense of being followed persisted, but she put it out of her mind. Hanging up her hat on a peg in the wall and casting her cloak over a chair, she lit a candle with flint and tinder, then sat at her dressing table to examine her prize. There was some kind of writing around the pot. For a time she puzzled over it. She had never learned to read, but it did not look like any letters she had ever seen. The face carved into the lid snarled up at her.

She wondered how much money she could get for the sale of the pot, and who might be interested in buying such an arcane and forbidden thing. The minister of the meeting house, Samuel Parris, was rumored to study the black arts in the privacy of his chambers, but she did not know how much trust to place in such tales. There was a Jew who traded up and down the coast – perhaps she could persuade him to part with a gold guinea for the salve. But first she must test it, to be certain the old woman had not lied to her. The suspicion began to grow in Moll's mind that she had been tricked, that the hag had slipped out a secret door in the back of the cabin and had followed her through the forest to the road, laughing at her.

She opened a shutter on the window and peered down at the road. The moonlight showed the wheel ruts in the frozen mud. The cart way between two houses opposite lay in deep shadow. She stared at it, not knowing what had attracted her eye, and saw the shadow move in a way that was not natural. It seemed to undulate and flow back between the two buildings like black smoke borne on a breeze. Then it was gone, leaving her to wonder if she had really seen it. Danvers Highlands that rose to the horizon beyond the houses was empty. She remembered that witches were rumored to have familiar demons to serve them and guard their dwelling places.

Drawing back from the window, she pulled the shutter in and latched it. Her eyes strayed back to the stone pot. She twisted it open, touched its milky-white contents with her fingers, and drew them alone the inside of her bare wrist. The ointment gleamed in the light of her candle, looking like nothing so much as a man's semen, a substance with which she was well familiar. It felt cooling against her skin and not unpleasant, although the odor was repugnant in a way she could not define. It made her stomach roll. When nothing happened, she spread more ointment over her other wrist. Still nothing. She resisted the sudden urge to open the shutters and throw the stone pot out the window.

The old woman had applied it to her entire body. With a shrug Moll stood, took off her red dress, and stepped out of her bumroll. She wore no stays. Pulling the simple white shift that served as an undergarment over her head, she stood naked save for her shoes and knitted white stockings. Her skin shone pale where the sun had never touched it. She no longer held any hope for the ointment, but she applied it to her calves, thighs, belly, buttocks, and breasts.

As she rubbed it into her hardened nipples with her palms, the room blurred and wavered, and the candle flame seemed to danced around her. She felt herself falling. With a rush of air she was carried toward the window. The shutters burst outward and she flew across the road, above the rooftops and over Danvers Highlands, her thin scream of mingled surprise and terror diminishing into the night stillness.

The shadow in the alley undulated, flowing together into a more compact mass of blackness. It rose up and floated across the road to the open window. For a few moments it flowed around the shutters, then it entered the room and settled over the stone pot of ointment on the table. It drifted back out the window and over the rooftops in the same direction Moll had been carried, moving ever faster until it merged with the starry sky.

3.

Stars whirled around her on silver streaks. Sometimes the moon was above her and sometimes below. It felt like falling a vast distance through the whistling crystal night but something bore her up and kept her flying through the wind, which was so cold that in a few moments her limbs went numb and her tears of terror froze on her cheeks. The thought came to her that she would soon be frozen stiff, like a slab of beef hung from a tree on a winter's night. Fear transformed to fury. She cursed God for serving her such a foul turn of fate.

The darkness around her became more tangible. It thickened and wrapped about her body, shielding her from the icy wind. She felt it tugging, pulling, guiding her through the air, and she did not attempt to resist. It was like a shadow that she could see through. The stars ceased to spin above and below her. The moonlight revealed that she was being carried high above jagged mountain peaks. After many minutes an enormous black mountain with a flat top loomed on the horizon. She found herself descending toward it.

Flecks of red gleamed from its hollowed crest. As she drew nearer she saw that they were bonfires. Smaller sparks danced around them. These were made by torches. The sound of revelry came to her ears, shouts and laughter and shrieks of delight, and with them the regular beating of drums and the shrill piping of flutes.

The transparent blackness that enfolded her set her down on a rough platform hewn out of the raw stone of the mountain, then left her there dizzy and staggering. It was elevated above the basin of the mountaintop. Looking down, she saw thousands of human beings in the firelight, dancing in rings with hands joined and backs turned to the bonfires. Some stood apart, drinking from flagons or feasting from bowls as they looked upon the scene. All were naked, and most of the men were rudely erect. On the rocky ground men coupled with women, women with women, men with men.

She discovered a set of steps carved into the rock and followed them downward. The heat from the fires was welcome on her naked limbs, but the noise of the drums and pipes along with the raucous bellowing of the crowd was almost painful. Never had she witnesses such a scene of unchecked mass debauchery. The expressions on the faces of men, women, even children, were twisted masks of madness. She walked among them clad only in shoes and stockings with her arms at her sides, and made no attempt to cover her nakedness. As a girl she had grown up on the London docks. Shame was a word that held no meaning for her. No one turned to stare at her or spoke. It was as though she went unseen.

At length she came upon a great cauldron of black iron hung over a cooking fire. Three old women were tending it. One sat stirring its bubbling contents with a long wooden ladle. Another stood at a stump, cutting up sections of raw meat with a cleaver. The third sat poking the fire with a stick, her back to Moll. Something on her shoulder moved and made a kind of chittering sound. The old woman turned, and Moll saw that it was Mother Wilde.

"I thought I might see ye here afore long."

"What is this place?" Moll asked.

"The sabbat meeting. What did ye think it were?"

"Then all these gathered here are witches?"

Mother Wilde cackled. "Witch is just a word, child. Church folk don't know what we be."

"I took your pot of ointment. I didn't think it would work."

The old woman nodded. "I expected as much. That's why I set Long Jim to watch for ye and guide ye here."

The creature on her shoulder chittered and bobbed its little head up and down. Moll stared at it but could not quite make out what kind of animal it might be. It was long and sleek like a weasel, but it seemed to have more than two eyes and more than four legs. A kind of black smoke hung around its fur and blurred its edges.

The old woman chopping the meat gathered the pieces in her withered fingers and carried them to the cauldron. She cast Moll a sly look from the corner of her eye as she passed.

"I want to go back to Salem Village. I don't belong here."

"Are ye so sure of that?"

"I'm not a witch."

"Would ye like to be one?"

Moll looked around at the debauchery and drunkenness. It was not far different from what she had seen in any number of bawdy houses, though on a larger scale both in size and extremity.

"I don't yet know. Mayhap. But I must learn how to go home."

Mother Wilde took her hand and gripped it when she tried to pull it away. She stared into Moll's green eyes.

"Ye must give an offering to Vass when ye are presented before him. If ye find favor in his sight, your wish will be granted."

Moll was finally able to twist her hand away. She spread her arms. "What gift can I give? I am naked. All I have are my shoes, and I doubt your god will want them."

"He's your god now, my girl," the old woman said.

She picked up a brown sack from the ground beside her and stood holding it dangling from her hand. Something inside the sack moved.

"I shall give ye your offering this time, since it is your first."

She carried the sack to the stump and dumped out its contents. A naked baby that could not have been more than a month old fell across the hacked surface and began to bawl. Moll saw that it was a boy.

"What are you doing?" she asked, looking around. But the revellers ignored them. One of the old women chuckled.

"There are few offerings to Vass that will insure the god's favor," Mother Wilde said. "One of them is the still-warm heart of a babe."

Moll looked down at the squalling infant. Her heart was moved with apprehension.

"What you speak of is murder. I want no part in a hanging crime."

"Look around ye. Do ye see a sheriff about? Or a judge? And even if there was one here that was such, do ye think he would arrest ye in this place?"

Moll considered these words as she gazed around. There was truth in them.

"Very well, get on with it."

"Oh no, my girl, that's not how it is done. This be your offering." She passed the meat cleaver to Moll, who took it with numb fingers.

The other two old women crept forward and surrounded the stump with Mother Wilde as Moll hesitated, staring down at the baby. It bleated and coughed a tiny cough, then gazed steadily up at her with blue eyes. Gathering her resolve, she raised the cleaver and chopped off its head with a single blow.

"Well struck," one of the old women said.

Swallowing down her disgust, Moll used the sharp edge of the cleaver to open the babe's breast and forced its ribs apart with her fingers, then with much fiddling managed to cut free its tiny heart, which she held out for the others to see. It was warm against her palm.

"The offerings are to begin," Mother Wilde said, glancing around. The drums had ceased to beat and the pipes had ceased to shrill. "Follow me, girl."

Most of the throng was shuffling in files in the same direction. Moll realized she was being led toward a pillar of black stone that jutted up from the ground. It was rough and irregular, and did not have the look of something carved by the hand of man. As she drew nearer, she realized how large it was. The rounded top hung high above her head.

The gathered crowd parted to let Mother Wilde lead her to its base. They had a hushed, watchful air. Moll wondered at so severe a change from their former mirth. A fire burned in a kind of stone trough at the base of the pillar, which extended over it at an angle. Moll suddenly realized that it resembled an erect penis both in its shape and its inclination.

"What must I do?" she whispered nervously.

"Ye must wish in your heart for the thing ye most want, and then cast your offering onto the embers. Then, if Vass wills it, ye must catch the drop of his seed in your hands as it falls and put it on your tongue."

The old woman stepped back, leaving her to stand alone under the looming darkness of the pillar.

She gathered her resolve and her courage, and fixed in her mind what she wanted. Take me back to the place I came from, she thought, and cast the tiny heart into the fire. It flared up and crackled on the bed of embers, and a plume of smoke arose and curled itself around the pillar.

Remembering the words of the old woman, Moll stepped back and cupped her hands. She looked up at the end of the pillar. There was complete stillness in the gathered crowd, which might almost have been composed of statues carved by some mad Greek sculptor.

Firelight gleamed on something at the tip of the pillar. It slowly grew in size, then without warning detached itself from the stone and fell. Moll almost misjudged its path, but corrected the placement of her cupped hands and managed to catch the pearly drop on her palms. She brought her hands to her face and licked them.

A cheer burst forth from the massed ranks around her. Suddenly the night was filled once again with shouts and laughter. The drums began to beat and the pipes to shrill.

Moll turned around where she stood, looking down at her body, then at Mother Wild, who stood some short distance away.

"It didn't work," she said. "Nothing is happening."

The old woman merely smiled and nodded her head, a gleam in her gray eyes. Moll blinked in amazement. Mother Wilde had begun to grow. As Moll watched, she became taller than a man, then as tall as a tree. Moll fell backward onto the ground. She tried to speak but only a kind of gurgling came from her throat.

Mother Wilde approached and towered over her, a giant of a woman. She bent and picked Moll up in her hands, then carried her between the bonfires. Moll stared from side to side. All of the witches had become giants. They cast knowing glances from the corners of their eyes as she was borne past. Moll felt herself laid gently onto a hard surface. Mother Wilde leaned over her with something in her hand.

"I can guess what ye wished for," the old woman said. "To go back from whence ye came. Most wish for it, then wish they hadn't. Ye should have wished to be made one with us. Well, there's no help for it now."

She raised her arm, and the last thing Moll saw was the meat cleaver, its blade stained with blood.

THE ROSE CIRCLE

Chapter 1: The Séance.

Two young women sat facing each other on a high-backed sofa, their knees touching, their hands clasped, their faces shining with excitement. The prettier of the two was tall and slender, dark-haired, with gray eyes and skin as white as milk. Her companion was brown of hair and eyes, shorter and a trifle plump. A spray of freckles crossed the bridge of her upturned nose.

"Isn't this thrilling?" the prettier one said. "A real séance in this house, with a medium from London. They say Madame French has given séances for Queen Victoria."

"It is exciting," the brown-haired girl agreed. "And perhaps just a little frightening."

"Don't tell me you're afraid of ghosts?"

"I am, though, just a little."

"Nonsense, Sarah. Everyone is having séances these days. It's all the rage."

"I'm surprised your mother agreed to it," Sarah said. "She's usually so strict."

An elderly woman sitting in the corner put down her needlepoint hoop and lowered the wire-framed spectacles on her long nose to peer over the top of them.

"It's Jane's doing," she said in a cracked voice of disapproval. "Whatever Miss Jane wants in this house, Miss Jane gets."

"Oh, really, Nanny," Jane Harwood said with a pout. "You make me sound like some kind of tyrant."

"I would never have agreed to it," the old woman said, adjusting the knitted wool shawl around her shoulders with petulant fingers. "But your mother is weak and easily swayed. No good will come of this night, mark my words."

As if to emphasize her dire prediction, a burning log in the fireplace collapsed and sent up a shower of sparks. Sarah jumped, then giggled nervously.

"Won't you be joining the séance, Nanny Harwood?" Sarah asked.

"I'll be there. Someone needs to keep discipline in this house."

"You're not going to spoil it, Nanny?" Jane said in alarm. "Please don't spoil it."

The old woman sniffed and went back to her needlepoint.

"Is Robert coming?" Sarah asked Jane.

"He promised he would be here if he could get away from the bank in time."

"He wasn't at home when I left."

As if on cue, a butler opened the doors of the drawing room.

"Mr. Robert Logan," he announced.

A young man in a business suit swept past him with a broad grin on his freckled face. He went directly to the sofa and kissed Jane on the cheek.

"Robert, you came. I'm so glad," she said.

"I hope I'm not late. I came straight here from the train station."

"The Frenches haven't arrived yet."

He knelt on the carpet before her, then glanced at the old woman, who kept her face fixed on her needlepoint. He took Jane's hand between his.

"You're really excited about this, aren't you?"

"How could I not be? I've been reading for months about Spiritualism and all the wonderful things that happen at séances. Did you know it all started the year I was born?"

"I know nothing whatsoever about it."

"It's true. A family in a little town in the state of New York started hearing ghostly raps all over their house, and the three young girls of the family talked to the spirits that made them. In only nineteen years it's spread all around the world. It's like Bible miracles come to life."

"You won't be too disappointed if nothing happens?"

"No. But I know something is going to happen tonight. I can feel it."

"Listen to your betrothed," Sarah told her brother. "She has the second sight."

He laughed gently. "You know I don't believe in such things."

"So you think it's all a fraud?" Jane asked in a hurt tone.

"Of course. What else could it be?"

Jane withdrew her hand. "Sometimes I don't think you believe in anything."

"I believe in you, Jane darling, and our future together as man and wife. Isn't that enough?"

Before she could answer, voices reached their ears from the front hall.

"That must be the Frenches," Sarah said.

"Let's go see them," Jane said, jumping to her feet.

When they reached the front hall, Jane's mother stood talking to a full-figured woman of middle years. Her bosom was impressive to the point of intimidation, accentuated as it was by her tightly laced corset. Beside her stood a mousy, balding little man with rounded shoulders, who held his hat in both hands by its brim. The butler gently removed the hat as the big woman's strident voice filled the hall.

"I'm delighted to be here, Mrs. Harwood. Delighted. The spirits have informed me this will be an auspicious night for materializations."

"Well, that is good to hear," Mrs. Harwood said. "My daughter is so looking forward to your performance."

"Perform? Perform? Oh no, Mrs. Harwood, I don't perform. I am a channel for higher beings. I provide them with a voice, that is all. I don't perform."

"Of course, Mrs. French. That was what I meant to say."

The big woman glanced at the little man. "Walter, go and see that the apparatus has been properly prepared."

"Yes, my love."

He followed the butler down the hall.

"Won't you come into the drawing room for a sherry before we begin?"

They filed into the drawing room the young people had just quitted and sat waiting while a maid poured drinks and set them on a tray. Mrs. French sipped her sherry with evident pleasure.

"It was a long carriage ride from Boston. Very dry, very dry indeed."

"You didn't take the train?" Robert said.

"No trains. Can't abide the things. Too modern. They upset the vibrations, you know."

"Please, do have another sherry," Mrs. Harwood said.

The maid refilled the medium's extended glass.

Jane noticed with a slight shock of surprise that the little finger was missing from the medium's left hand.

Mrs. French cast her bird-like eyes around the room. The old woman in the corner kept her gaze on her needlework.

"Is this everyone who will be at the table?"

"It is."

"Not your husband, then?"

"Mr. Harwood passed away a year ago. I'm afraid we won't be seeing him tonight."

"Don't be so certain of that," Mrs. French said. "I am well acquainted with the skeptical attitude, but you must believe. Best not to have skeptics at the table – it creates a barrier, you know."

Jane glanced at her fiancé, but said nothing.

They chatted about inconsequential things for a time. Mrs. French set her glass down and stood.

"Shall we go in now? I feel that the spirits are ready."

"Yes, certainly," said Mrs. Harwood, rising. "Follow me, everyone."

They filed through the hall and entered the library. The servants had moved a heavy round table on a pedestal into the center of the room and arranged chairs around it. In a corner of the room stood a cabinet of Japanned panels that bore a floral design. On a side table near the cabinet had been placed a trumpet, a tambourine, a guitar, and a small mirror. The trumpet was a simple cone of brass open at both ends, and did not appear to be something from which anyone could extract a musical note.

"What is that?" Robert whispered to Jane.

"They call it a spirit cabinet. The medium sits in it. You'll see."

The little man came forward with several lengths of white cord in his hands.

"I know there are skeptics among us," boomed Mrs. French. "There are always skeptics. To prove to you all that no trickery is involved,

Walter will bind my wrists and ankles to the chair inside the spirit cabinet. It will be impossible for me to rise from the chair until these bonds have been untied."

"Is that really necessary?" asked Mrs. Harwood.

"I must insist on it," the medium said.

At her invitation, they gathered around the cabinet to examine it. All its sides seemed solid, except for a small sliding hatch in the front panel. The entire panel opened on hinges like a door to admit the occupant. There was no roof on the structure. They watched the little man bind his wife's ankles to the legs of a plain wooden chair in which she sat. Her wrists were tied behind her back.

"Walter will bind up my mouth so that I cannot speak during the proceedings."

He took a white cloth from his pocket and tied it around his wife's head so that it passed between her upper and lower teeth. He closed the cabinet, and slid open the hatch to examine her.

"Come and see," he said in a small voice.

One by one, they peered into the cabinet through the open hatch, and saw the medium, still bound hand and foot, and gagged. Her eyes were shut.

"Let us assume our places at the table," Walter said. "As much as possible, it is best to alternate the sexes. This balances the astral forces involved."

He took his seat. Jane sat on one side of him, and Sarah on the other. Robert sat beside Jane. Mrs. Harwood and her mother-in-law took the remaining chairs.

"The lights must be put out," Walter French said. "There must be total darkness. Light is fatal to physical manifestations."

"The windows have been covered, as you directed in your letter," Mrs. Harwood told him. "No light can get into this room."

"Very good. Now join hands and close the circle."

They grasped hands on the table top, and Mrs. Harwood nodded to the butler, who used a candle snuffer to put out, one by one, the candles burning in a candelabra on the mantle. The fire had not been lit. As the last candle failed, absolute darkness took possession of the room.

They sat in silence. The darkness magnified small sounds. Each heard the breathing of the others, the scrap of a shoe on the floor, the ticking of the ceramic clock on the mantle. When Jane swallowed, it sounded loud in her own ears. Robert's hand was cool in hers, but the hand of Mr. French was hot and had begun to sweat.

"We are gathered here to receive evidence of the spirit realm," French said in his small, precise voice. "Is a spirit present within this room? If so, give us a sign of your presence."

Nothing happened. They waited. The little man repeated his words more insistently. The silence lengthened.

Robert leaned his head toward Jane. "This is all nonsense –"

A loud bang came from the underside of the table. They all flinched.

"Maintain contact," French told them. "If you value your lives, do not break the circle."

Jane heard a small voice in the distance. It sounded like the voice of a little girl, and she was singing a nursery rhyme.

"Mary had a little lamb, whose fleece was white as snow ..."

"Who is present?" French demanded.

"Lucy," the voice said.

"Lucy, do you have a message for the people gathered here?"

"All is well," said the voice. "All is as it should be."

A musical note suddenly blared out from the darkness. Something floated in the air above their heads. It was indistinct, and seemed to glow with an inner light. Jane realized that it was the trumpet that had been resting on the side table. Another blaring note sounded from it, and then it vanished. She heard the strings of the guitar plucked one by one.

Two more loud knocks came from the table. Jane could feel it jumping under her hands. Slowly, the table began to tilt. It maintained its angle for several seconds, then dropped back to the floor with a thud.

"Have you anything more to show us, spirit?" French asked in a quavering voice.

"Look, there, by the cabinet," Sarah whispered.

Jane turned and saw a faint glow upon the air. It bobbed and floated, gradually becoming larger and assuming the distinct shape of a human head and shoulders. It was the image of a young girl with long, flowing hair. She looked down at them and seemed to smile wanly.

"What have you to tell us, Lucy?" French asked.

"One has been chosen," said the little girl's voice.

"Chosen in what way? Do you mean someone from this circle?"

"Yes. She has been chosen for great enlightenment."

"Who chose her, Lucy?"

"Our Father chose her."

"What is her name?"

The apparition parted its lips and seemed about to speak. Abruptly, it vanished.

"Lights," Walter French said.

The butler, who all this while had stood beside the fireplace, struck a match against its bricks and ignited the candles in the candelabra one by one until the room glowed. French released the hands of the girls and went quickly to the spirit cabinet, which he flung open with a somewhat theatrical gesture. There was Mrs. French, still sitting bound and gagged in her chair. Her eyes were closed and her head lolled against her shoulder. Her husband laid his hand gently on her knee, which caused her to start and open her eyes. He untied her gag and she licked her lips.

"What happened?" she demanded.

"Manifestations, my dear," the little man said. "Very satisfying manifestations indeed."

They went into the drawing room for another round of drinks. The butler served *hors d'oeuvre* on a silver tray. Water chestnuts, wrapped in strips of bacon. Mrs. French seemed especially to enjoy them.

"It was the most wonderful thing I have ever seen," Mrs. Harwood told the medium. "Absolutely astonishing."

"A minor demonstration of the power of the spirits, nothing more."

"If I may ask," Robert said. "What is your role in the séance?"

"I shine on the astral plane," Mrs. French told him. "I am like a beacon in the darkness. The spirits are drawn to me, and through me they are enabled to communicate with you."

"Yes, but what do you actually do? Is it you blowing the trumpet?"

The grandmother snorted suppressed laughter.

"You are an impertinent young man," the medium said, glaring at him.

"Robert, how could you?" Jane said in distress. "Forgive him, Madame

French. He's not a believer."

"Lack of faith is its own punishment, belief its own reward," she said. "He knows not what he speaks."

"Don't mind me," he said. "You ladies enjoy yourselves."

"I think we will be going now," Mrs. French said.

They stood and accompanied the medium into the hall, where coats and hats were provided by servants. Jane deliberately distanced herself from her fiancé. She felt mortified by his behavior. She found herself close to the medium, who was settling an enormous hat with a broad brim onto her head. From it jutted a blue ostrich feather. Jane's gaze fell on something white that hung from her handbag. She realized it was a piece of cheesecloth. The medium saw where she was looking and tucked the cloth back into the bag.

"You are a true believer," Mrs. French told Jane. "And you have the gift. I sense it within you. But you must bring it forth or it will wither and die. Here, take this card. There is a lecture being given at Edwards Hall in Boston on Thursday at eight o'clock. This card will gain you admittance. I urge you to attend. That is all I have to say."

The couple departed the house without uttering another word. They climbed into the waiting carriage and were gone.

Chapter 2: The Lecture

"If we don't hurry, we'll be late," Jane said anxiously.

"I could order the driver to lash the horses into a gallop," Robert told her with a wry smile.

"On crowded Boston streets? That would hardly do," Sarah said.

"Thank you for escorting us to the lecture, Robert. I know how little you believe in Spiritualism," Jane said.

"Don't be silly. There's nowhere else I'd rather be than with you."

"We couldn't have come without you," Sarah said. "It wouldn't have been proper."

It was not yet eight o'clock but already dark. The wheels of their carriage clattered down a narrow street over dirty cobblestones. Jane glanced out the open window and saw a derelict raise a bottle to his lips. A robust woman in a red dress made some kind of rude gesture at him and laughed loudly. It sounded like the braying of a donkey. In an instant the street tableau was left behind. This was a part of Boston she had never seen before. Boarded up shops and houses with peeling paint and broken windows flashed past.

The carriage stopped in front of a dilapidated theater. There were no lights or signs to indicate a lecture was to take place within. Tattered theatrical posters fluttered on a display board, an indication of more prosperous times. A rough-looking man in a bowler hat stood to one side of the entrance. Robert leaned his head out a window.

"Are you sure this is the correct address?" he asked the coachman.

"It's the address Miss Harwood gave me, sir. Edwards Hall."

"Let me get out and talk to that man," Robert said.

Jane watched him cross the street and argue with the man at the door, who shook his head several times. He came back to the coach.

"He says he won't let us in," he explained through the window.

"Is there not to be a lecture?" Sarah asked.

"He wouldn't say. He just refused to admit us."

"Let me try," Jane said impulsively.

Before Robert could object, she stepped from the carriage and walked briskly toward the man, who now stood in front of the double theater doors with his burly arms crossed on his chest. Robert trailed behind her.

"It was our understanding, sir, that a lecture was to be given in this theater tonight at eight o'clock."

The man stared at her without speaking, a slight smirk on his lips. A scar across his cheek glowed in the light from the nearest gas lamp like a splash of white paint.

"I was given this card of entry by Madam Leda French. Perhaps you've heard of her?"

He peered at the card and grunted, then reluctantly stepped aside and opened one side of the double doors.

"I'm going in," she said to her fiancé, suppressed excitement in her voice. "Fetch Sarah, would you, Robert?"

Robert cast a hard look at the doorman.

"You're not going to get much trade this way, my good fellow."

"Go chase yourself," the man said in a rough voice.

Jane waited in the entrance hall until Robert and Sarah joined her. The three proceeded into the depths of the theater. It was lighted dimly. The air hung heavy with a rich odor of sweat and tobacco. They came to an inner set of doors and heard murmuring on the other side.

"I'm no longer sure this is a good idea," Robert said. "That fellow at the door was a rum sort. Did you see that scar on his face?"

"One could scarcely miss it," Jane said, and pushed the doors open.

The theater was small, but at one time in its history must have been elegant. Carved woodwork of flowering vines and cherub faces gleamed around the elevated box seats, their gilding still intact in places, and the seat backs of the chairs on the floor were of red velvet. The air hung heavy with the smoke of cigars. It was not a large theater, but only about half its seats were occupied by men and women from various classes of society. Most of them were seated near the stage, which had a brown curtain across it. They found places in a row behind the others and sat.

"I don't like this," Robert murmured. "These aren't our sort of people."

A young woman in a loose white dress open at the neck, her honey-blonde hair cut short and curling in the Bohemian fashion, walked onto the stage from one of the wings. There was no applause.

"Father will give a talk. Then we shall perform the sun ceremony." Her voice was small but clear.

She walked back across the stage the way she had come.

In the silence, the squeak of a pulley was audible as the curtain lifted. A man stood center stage. He was above the middle height and broad in the shoulders, but his face was uncommonly thin, his cheeks hollow. It was the face of an ascetic. He wore a curious blue silk robe with various arcane symbols embroidered on it that was tied tight at his waist with a multicolored sash. Outlined in gold cloth on each breast of the robe was the Egyptian symbol of an eye. On his head rested a white leather cap that came down to cover his neck and ears, and in his hands he held the long stem of a white lily. The silence lengthened for more than a full minute.

"There are no accidents," the man said. "You have been chosen."

His voice, although not raised above the conversational level, filled the entire theater. The air resonated with his words. Black eyeliner made his pale, watery-blue eyes stand forth from his thin face in a startling manner.

He looked directly at Jane as he spoke, and a thrill ran through her from the soles of her feet to the roots of her hair. She knew, without the least doubt, that he was speaking to her, and that no one else mattered.

"We are Azarial. We bring you greetings from the Summerland. We have been sent to this vessel of flesh to instruct you in the things of the spirit. This burden we bear gladly for the sake of your soul.

"Tonight, we speak on the nature of spirit. What is spirit? It is a breath, is it not? The *pneuma* of the Greeks, the *spiritus* of the Romans. On an inhalation of breath you entered this life, and on an exhalation you shall leave it. Yet this breath is not a formless thing. Its manifestations are too many to be conceived. When spirit becomes differentiated, it gains awareness of itself. The greatest spirits are sparks struck forth from the anvil of light. These are the spirits of the higher planes, of whom we are one. You call us angels and other such names. We have spoken to you as two conjoined minds, but now a spirit within this flesh will speak to you alone.

"You must forsake your old beliefs and come to us."

Several members of the audience drew startled breaths. The voice of the speaker had changed, not just in intonation and pitch, but in sex. It was the liquid, flowing voice of a woman who spoke from the man's throat in a vibrant contralto.

"It's a trick," Robert murmured to Jane.

"Shush," she said, leaning forward.

"You are never alone. We are always with you. We stood at the bedside of your mother when you are born, and will be at your sick bed when you die. Yet you continue to deny us entry into your mind, into your heart, into your flesh. You lead your empty, lonely life, bereft of true friendships, forsaken in love, while all the time we stand next to you, ever ready to give you our friendship, our love."

"I think we should leave," Robert whispered. "This is not a Christian message."

"I want to hear him – her," Jane corrected herself.

"My name is not important," the female voice said. "The birth name of this vessel of flesh is not important. Together we are Azarial. We know neither sorrow nor fear. We can show you the way to become as we are if you will follow in our footsteps. Nothing is forbidden you. Nothing is impossible. There is no sin, only death. But when you become as we are, death holds no terror, only bliss. Death is a doorway through which you will walk into a more enlightened existence in the Summerland. There you will dwell amid green fields and crystal streams, where flowers bloom and the sun is always shining.

"Walk with me, my child. I am the way and the light. Let me free you from your worldly cares. What have you to lose, except your fear? Why do you cling with such desperation to fear, when it is but a cold stone that will pull you ever downward into the waters of oblivion? For us, death is but a portal that opens on a world of eternal sunshine, but for the fearful, death is the end of all; death is endless darkness, the yawning jaws of nothingness that will consume you. I beg you, my child, cast off your fears and join us."

As he spoke, several young women in white dresses moved among the audience with wooden bowls in their hands, collecting coins much in the same way as might have been done in church during services. One came near to where they sat, and with a grunt of disapproval, Robert dug into his pocket and came up with a silver dollar. The golden-haired girl, who could not have been more than sixteen years of age, smiled at him.

"Now can we get out of here?" he asked Jane when the girl withdrew.

Sarah leaned in from Jane's opposite side. "There's still some kind of performance that is supposed to take place, I think."

"I want to stay and see it all, Robert. We might as well, since we're here anyway."

The man calling himself Azarial finished speaking and stood motionless while the brown curtain was lowered in front of him. The young woman with the Bohemian hair style who had introduced him returned in front of the curtain.

"Now we will perform the ceremony of the sun. Father Azarial has instructed me to tell you that this is a rare privilege your enjoy. Few outsiders have ever witnessed this ceremony."

She left the stage. After a few moments, a violin began to play. It gave forth slow, dreamlike notes of a melody unlike any Jane had ever heard. The nasal sound of an obo joined the violin, and for a few minutes the two instruments produced music that danced and entwined in a sensual manner. A brass gong sounded. The curtain squeaked up.

The stage was dark, filled with shadows and cold light that simulated moonlight. The backdrop showed a forest scene. Center stage was occupied by a low oblong structure painted to resemble a recumbent stone altar. A solitary woman in a black robe whose dark hair hung down almost to her waist stood in a sorrowful posture, her back to the moonlight, her head bowed. Strident chords came from the unseen violin. She began a melancholy dance around the altar.

The Bohemian woman who had introduced the night's entertainment stood to one side, similarly robed in black.

"The dance of despair," she said in a dramatic voice. "The soul is lost in darkness and cannot find escape. No matter where it turns, there are more shadows."

Suddenly with the clash of brass gongs, a dark figure arose at the rear of the stage. Like the dancer, the figure wore a black robe, but its head was covered by a hood. In its hands it carried a scythe. Jane could not determine if it was a man or a woman. It was big enough to be a man, but seemed to have a woman's hips. This figure stepped slowly forward and began to pass the blade of the scythe over the head of the dancer, who vainly attempted to evade the strokes.

"Death comes to her, as it comes to all who live in fear and darkness. Death, the end of her despair."

The dancer reeled and fell back to lie upon the low gray altar, which was in this way transformed into her funeral bier. The figure of Death lowered its scythe and approached the altar, then bent down to kiss the reclining dancer on the lips. Its overhanging hood concealed the actual contact from the audience.

Lightening flashed in the background, and thunder crashed. It blinded the audience momentarily. When they could see once again, the dancer had cast off her black robe. She stood upon the altar clothed in a long white gown of some diaphanous material that revealed her nakedness beneath it. Death had vanished, replaced by an elevated throne on which sat a bearded man dressed Roman-style in a toga, with vine leaves twined around his head into a kind of crown. Gradually the light strengthened into a simulation of golden sunlight. It was Azarial, but so transformed as to be hardly recognizable.

"Death holds no terror for the enlightened soul, which cannot die but lives forever in the Summerland," the Bohemian woman recited.

Four young women appeared, two from each side of the stage, as the music became cheerful and lilting. They wore pleated white dresses that came to just below their knees. Their feet were bare, their breasts exposed. Jane glanced at Robert and saw his jaw tighten in anger, but he said nothing.

The four dancers began to strew the stage with rose petals from baskets they carried. Around and around the altar they danced, then set aside their baskets and helped the woman who stood on the alter climb down, escorting her up the steps to the throne. The woman who had died and been reborn began to make yearning gestures toward the seated man, but he failed to give any sign that he noticed her. The four dancers sang in a wordless crooning, and seemed to implore him to show mercy. At last the woman fell to her knees and clasped the leg of the seated man. She reached up to stoke his beard, then rested her head on his knee. He finally lowered his gaze to her and placed his hand upon her head.

"The soul is accepted into the Summerland by its benevolent lord," the Bohemian chorus of one recited. "Happy is this day, from now unto eternity."

The four bare-breasted dancers whirled and danced in a circle before the throne as the music of the violin and obo achieved a kind of climax and died away. The curtain slowly descended.

There was scattered applause from the audience. People began to stand up and file toward the central aisle.

"It must be over," Sarah said. "I thought it would never end."

"It was smut," Robert said. "Let's get out of here."

"I have to talk to him," Jane said, her eyes shining with emotion.

Robert stared at her with incomprehension. "Are you serious?"

"Take me back stage, Robert."

"I certainly will not. Those women were half-naked. They should all be arrested for public indecency."

He began to draw Jane toward the aisle, but she resisted.

"If you won't escort me, I shall go alone."

"Jane, you can't," Sarah said. "Those people are all insane. They may be dangerous."

"The man looked like a dope fiend," Robert said.

"How would you know what a dope fiend looks like?" Jane demanded.

"Well, anyway, he's not normal."

They reached the aisle. Most of the audience had left the theater. Instead of moving toward the exit, Jane made her way down toward the stage.

"Jane, I forbid it."

She did not stop.

"Go out and wait for us in the coach," Robert told his sister.

"Are you going with her?"

"I can't let her go alone."

"Maybe I should come too."

"No, Sarah. You've seen enough. We all have. I need to keep her safe."

He hurried after his fiancé, who passed through a door beside the stage. By the time he caught up with her, she was talking to an elderly man in a carpenter's apron. He gave her directions to the dressing rooms. Robert caught her arm.

"Jane, I'm asking you to come out of this place with me. These people are wrong. Their ideas aren't Christian."

"You go if you must," she said in a serene tone. "This is something I have to do."

He followed her silently to an open doorway, where she stopped to look inside the room beyond. A man sat in a dressing gown before a cracked mirror. He was applying cream to his face to remove the black makeup around his eyes. A false beard lay on the table. Robert realized it was the man on stage who had called himself Azarial.

Jane knocked timidly on the open door. The man glanced toward her, then stopped what he was doing and held her gaze with his eyes.

"You may sit over there," he told her, gesturing at an old sofa.

Robert started to enter behind her.

"Not you," Azarial said in a commanding tone that stopped the young man like a blow.

"Wait outside the door, Robert. I won't be long," Jane told him.

Robert's face flushed in anger. He clenched his hands into fists and sent a murderous look toward the seated man.

"Close the door behind you," the man told him.

After a moment, Robert stepped back out of the dressing room. The door slammed shut.

Azarial finished cleaning his face. Jane sat with her hands folded in her lap, waiting in silence.

"You are patient," he said at last. "That is good."

He stood and went to a table, where he poured himself a brandy from a decanter. He did not offer her any, but stood studying her profile with faded blue eyes.

"You were sent to me."

"Yes," she said without looking at him.

"You have the gift of sight."

"I – I don't know. Perhaps."

"You have the gift of sight. You are an old soul. You and I have known one another many time through the centuries. Sometimes you have been the teacher, and sometimes the pupil."

"I wish to learn."

He crossed to an ancient and battle-scarred desk and took from one of its drawers a book. Setting down his brandy, he wrote something on the flyleaf with a fountain pen and shut the book with a snap. He extended the book to her as she stood up.

"Read this. If you are still interested, come to me."

She approached slowly, unable to break eye contact with him. Her heart thudded inside her breast. Timidly, she took the book. He turned his back upon her. After a moment of silence, she left him.

"What did he say to you?" Robert demanded.

"Nothing. Everything."

"What on earth does that mean?"

"I don't want to talk now. Please take me home. I have a headache."

She said nothing more as they made their way from the theater to the waiting coach.

Chapter 3: The Book

"It's all my fault," Mrs. Harwood said, wringing her hands together. "If I hadn't agreed to the séance none of this would have happened."

She sat down on the edge of a chair, a worried expression lining her usually serene face. Sarah Logan was sitting on the sofa facing her. In her usual corner of the drawing room, the old woman silently did needlepoint. A fire crackled on the hearth.

"She barely talks to me these days," Sarah said. "It's that book. She spends all her time studying it."

"Do you know what's in it?"

Sarah shook her head. "She won't let me read it. She says I'm not ready."

"She won't let me see it, either. She hides it where I can't find it."

"Everything was fine until she was given that book."

The older woman shook her head and stared into the fire for a time. "Robert came to see her yesterday. She turned him away. I don't think she still wants to marry him."

"She's obsessed with that book," Sarah said. "She does strange rituals she's learned from it."

"What kind of rituals?" asked Mrs. Harwood.

"I don't know. She makes signs in the air with her hands. Pentacles of some kind. And she's doing breathing exercises. I'm afraid she might hurt herself."

"You're her dearest friend, Sarah. Can't you make her see how foolishly she is behaving? All this Spiritualism nonsense has gone to her head. It's like a mania. I'm afraid she may have to be committed."

"I'm sure it won't come to that," Sarah said, but there was no certainty in her voice.

"What are you two talking about?" Jane asked from the open doorway.

"We were just saying that we don't see enough of Robert these days," Mrs. Harwood said. "You should invite him to dinner, Jane."

Her daughter gave no answer. She stood in the doorway, staring past the two women as though looking at something in the distance that only she could see.

"Jane? About Robert."

Jane blinked and met her mother's worried gaze. "I'll invite him tonight, if you like."

"You must stay too, Sarah," Mrs. Harwood said.

"Yes, stay Sarah. My mother wishes you to."

"You've cut your hair."

Jane turned on her heel. "Do you like it?"

"It's very … Bohemian."

"What's the point in living in the past, when every day our lives march away from the past into the future?"

"You're not turning into an anarchist, I hope," Sarah said with a laugh.

"Well I don't know. I never thought of it that way, but perhaps I am."

The other women exchanged glances. The face of Jane's mother was heavy with sadness.

"I must go to the library and write a note inviting Robert for dinner," Jane said, and left the room.

"You see how it is?" Mrs. Harwood said. "I'm at my wits end."

"She is greatly changed since the last time I saw her," Sarah agreed.

"She's got the devil in her, and no mistake," said the old woman, who had watched all that passed in silence.

Mrs. Harwood rose from her chair and went to Sarah, who also stood. The older woman took the girl's hand.

"Will you do something for me?"

"Of course. What is it?"

"I want you to go to Jane's bedchamber and get that evil book. I will distract her in the library."

Sarah hesitated before answering.

"What you ask is a great deal – to betray Jane's trust in such a way."

"I saw her open the book once," the older woman said. "There was something written in pen on the flyleaf. I was not close enough to read what is said, but it was a man's handwriting."

"Do you think it might have significance in the way Jane has changed?"

"I think it may be the address of the person who gave her the book. If I know his address, I can have him investigated, and perhaps discouraged from future communications with her."

The imploring expression on the face of the older woman decided Sarah.

"I'll look for the book, and bring it to you if I find it."

"Then go quickly up the stairs while I delay Jane in the library."

Sarah followed Mrs. Harwood into the hall and ran lightly up the stairs.

She hurried to Jane's bedchamber, opened the door and slipped inside, wondering how long she should search for the book if it were hidden. But she saw it almost at once, sitting on top of the bureau, a slender octavo volume bound in black leather. She swept it up and hurried out of the room, holding the book concealed behind her back. The hall was empty. Tip-toeing down the stair, she returned to the drawing room.

"So you got the devilish thing," the old woman said, peering at Sarah over her spectacles.

Sarah blushed. She sat on the sofa and hid the book behind a cushion. In a few minutes, Mrs. Harwood entered. Her face was flushed and stern. It was obvious that her conversation with Jane had not gone well.

"Did you get it?"

Sarah slid the book from behind the cushion and extended it to her. Mrs. Harwood took it eagerly and opened it, then made a sound of frustration.

"The flyleaf has been torn out."

Sarah went to her and examined the book as the older woman leafed through its pages. There were strange diagrams and pentacles. Much of the text was in Latin, some of it in Greek. She wondered what Sarah could have made of it all.

Mrs. Harwood snapped the book shut. She went to the fireplace with purposeful steps and threw the book onto the embers. In moments it flared up and began to burn.

"Good," the old woman said.

Robert arrived shortly before six o'clock. He cut a handsome figure in his swallow-tailed dinner jacket and black tie. Mrs. Harwood guided him into the drawing room where Sarah sat reading a periodical. She put it down and smiled in greeting.

"How is Jane?" he asked with concern. "She hasn't let me see her for more than two weeks."

Sarah glanced at Mrs. Harwood. "We are worried about her behavior, Robert. Did you know she cut her hair?"

"No. Has she really?"

They nodded solemnly.

"She had such beautiful hair," he said.

"Hair is the least of your worries," the old woman said from the corner.

147

"You must try to draw her out over dinner," Mrs. Harwood told him. "Get her talking about her Spiritualist interests. We must discover who is influencing her."

"I can tell you that, at least," he said. "It's that charlatan whose lecture we attended last month. What was his name, Sarah?"

"Az something. Azarial, I think."

"But what is his real name?" Mrs. Harwood said impatiently. "Where does he live?"

The butler entered. "Dinner is served, madam."

"We'll go in," Mrs. Harwood told him. "Send a maid to fetch Miss Jane from her bedchamber."

Jane came into the dining room after they had seated themselves. She wore a loose blue peasant dress that was open at the shoulders. Robert stood while she took a chair across the table from him.

"Is that the most appropriate dress you could find for dinner?" her mother asked sharply.

Jane looked calmly at her mother, seated at the table's head. "Yes, it is."

"I would like you to say grace this evening."

Jane glanced around the table. A slight smile played over her lips. She pressed her palms together and closed her eyes.

"For what we are about to receive, we thank the spirits of the Summerland, who watch over us and are ever-present with us as our teachers and guides. Amen."

She opened her eyes and saw shock on the faces staring at her. Mrs. Harwood banged her hand down on the table with such force, the china rattled.

"That was blasphemous!"

"You asked me to say grace. You didn't specify what words I must use."

The meal was served. They ate in tense silence, all but Jane who seemed completely at her ease. During the final course, she tapped her crystal water glass with her desert spoon.

"I have an announcement to make. Well, two announcements actually, the second of which is more important than the first."

The others at the table regarded her in silence, their silverware suspended.

"First, my marriage to Robert Logan will not take place."

"Jane, what are you saying?"

"I'm sorry, Robert, but I no longer wish to become your wife."

"But, why? Have I done something to displease you?"

"Not really. It's simply that I have ascended above your level. Spiritually, I mean. We could never be happy together."

"Jane, let us go aside and talk about this."

She ignored his words. "My second announcement is that I shall be leaving this house to live elsewhere, with some friends."

"You can't leave," her mother said. "You're not of age."

"You're wrong. I can go wherever I choose to go. I have been liberated in spirit and will no longer be told what to do and what not to do."

Her mother's face twisted in anger.

"You won't be leaving with your precious book," she said in triumph.

"What did you do? Burn it?" The look in her mother's eyes made Jane laugh. "I don't need the book, mother. I don't need anything anymore. Don't you understand? The spirits have freed me. I walk among them as their equal. They talk to me at night before I fall asleep. They come to me in my dreams."

"You're speaking wildly, Jane," Sarah said gently. "Perhaps if you talked to a physician …"

Jane looked around the table and shook her head sadly. "You are all so limited in your thinking. I would stay and help you if I thought you would listen to my teachings, but I know you would not. I must attend to my own soul. I go to live with one who can advance me upon the higher planes, and who will teach me how to put my abilities to their best use."

"You'll go without money," her mother said, a spiteful note in her voice. "You'll go with the clothes on your back and not a penny in your purse."

"I have no need for money. Arrangement have already been made. When I am settled, I will write to you so that you know there is nothing to fear. Until then, do not worry about me. All is unfolding as it should."

She rose from the table and left the dining room. Her mother burst into tears. Sarah reached across the table and held the older woman's hand. Robert sat staring at the empty chair she had vacated, his face expressionless.

The grandmother set down her desert spoon with a clatter and licked cream from her wrinkled lips.

"Selfish girl," she said.

Chapter 4: The House

The house was called Briary Place. It was a rambling manor house of stone and red brick set on acres of rolling meadows surrounded by forest. It was difficult to believe it was almost on the outskirts of Boston. It gave the impression of another time, another world. The carriage came to a stop on the gravel circle opposite the front door. Jane got out and stood gazing up at the tall windows and ornamental chimney pots.

Wings of the house extended on either side, but the wing on the right looked cleaner and better maintained. On the left wing the paint of the white window frames was peeling, which gave it a neglected appearance. Some distance away stood a carriage house. The grass on the front lawn was in need of cutting, the flowering shrubs on either side of the entrance way had grown wild, and one of several vines climbing the face of the building had died.

The carriage driver unloaded her bags and put them on the front step beside the door. Jane watched him drive away with a clatter of hooves on stones. After spending several moments admiring the view across lawn, at the edge of which there was a small pond with shade trees and a summer house, she grasped an ornate brass knocker shaped in the grinning, leaf-shrouded face of the Green Man of the forest, and used it to give four sharp raps on the door. Then she waited.

The door opened. Jane stepped back involuntarily. The woman who had opened it was enormous. Not that she appeared corpulent, but she stood well over six feet in height and had a solid barrel of a body. She wore a conservative black dress that resembled a dress of mourning, save for its lack of black crepe. Her face was as square as her body, with a broad brow and a massive chin. Dark hair hung lifelessly down on either side of it, cut short before it reached her broad shoulders. Small black eyes set deep in their sockets stared down at Jane without expression. They reminded Jane of the eyes of a snake.

"I'm Jane Harwood."

The woman made no response.

"I'm expected."

Still nothing.

"Azarial invited me."

At the mention of his name, the woman's eyes suddenly opened wide, causing them to flash with black fire. She stepped back to allow Jane to enter.

"My bags," Jane said, pointing at her two cases.

The silent woman gave no indication that she had understood. After a moment, Jane bent and picked up the cases herself. She followed the woman into an entrance hall. An elderly man with a bent back and a nervous expression approached them. He wore the somewhat old-fashioned attire of a butler. The big woman gestured for Jane to set her cases down. She snapped her fingers and pointed at the man, then pointed at the cases, then up the stairs. The old man hurried over to pick up the cases. He seemed to cringe around the big woman, almost as though afraid to pass too near her.

The woman motioned for Jane to follow, and led Jane to a set of double doors, which she opened. Jane entered a library that at one time must have been a glorious thing, but now half the shelves that climbed from the oak floor to the lofty ceiling were empty and the great Persian carpet that almost covered the floor was worn and ragged at its edge.

A young woman who sat sideways in an arm chair, her bare legs dangling over one of the arms, set down the book she was reading and jumped to her feet. Jane recognized her as the woman with the curling honey-blonde hair who had introduced the entertainment at Edwards Hall. She had broad but not unattractive features and extraordinary ice-blue eyes that laughed when she smiled, as she did now.

"You must be Jane Harwood. We've all been expecting you. My name is Cynthia Fitzsimmons-Smythe, but everyone calls me Cyn."

She extended her hands and Jane clasped them warmly. With a slight start of surprise, she realized the small finger was missing from Cyn's left hand. She remembered the missing finger of Madame French and wondered at the coincidence, which seemed almost providential.

Cyn glanced up at the big woman, who stood as immobile as a statue.

"Thank you, Miss Voor. I'll introduce Miss Harwood to the rest of the household."

Miss Voor turned and left, closing the doors after her. The two women looked at each other. Then both giggled like school girls.

"What do you think of our Miss Voor?"

"She is certainly quite …" Jane found herself searching for words. "Quite … quite …"

"Big?" the other woman said. "She is huge. Enormous. Gigantic. She is a monster of a woman."

"Is she a servant?"

"Not in a formal sense. But she does run the entire household for Father and the rest of us. I don't know what we'd do without her, to be honest."

"Why is she so silent?"

"She can't speak. Not a word."

Stepping forward, she threw her arms around Jane and kissed her on the lips. Jane stared at her with startled eyes, struggling to remain composed.

"You are one of us now. We are a big family here. No formalities between us. We women are like sisters, and the men are like brothers. Come, let me introduce you to the others."

Putting her arm around Jane's waist, she guided her into the hall and down its length. They passed the open door of a drawing room. Jane saw an old woman sitting in a wingback chair before the fireplace, which was not lit. She had a shawl clutched around her shoulders and sat hunched forward, staring into the cold fireplace, her jaw trembling.

Cyn noticed Jane looking into the room.

"That's old Mrs. Reeves. She owns this house. But don't pay any attention to her, none of us do."

They entered a games room with a billiard table in the center of the floor. Two young men in shirtsleeves were playing billiards while a more slightly built third man, immaculately dressed in a gray suit with a white carnation in its lapel, stood idly watching. The pair at the table paused their game and came forward for introductions.

"This is Teddy Reeves, old Mrs. Reeves grandson, and his friend Sean O'Conner. Each gave a small bow of his head at his name. Teddy was a short, plump man in his mid-twenties with a boyish face. Sean was athletic, taller and broad in the shoulders. His face had that shadow of a beard that men with very dark hair seem to perpetually wear, even when they shave daily.

"Welcome to my humble abode," Teddy said. His voice was slurred.

"The more, the merrier," Sean said with a broad Irish accent.

The third man, who was older than these two by at least a decade, stepped away from the wall he had been leaning against.

"Must I introduce myself?" he asked with a slight lisp. "How gauche."

Cyn pursed her lips in irritation as she looked at him. "This is Cyril James, our resident dilettante."

"We're all dilettante here, darling," Cyril told her with a lift of his thin eyebrows.

"Cyril likes to think of himself as an artist," Teddy explained. "He produced that entertainment you saw at the Edwards Hall."

"It was beautiful," Jane told the thin man, who blushed at her words.

"Unsolicited praise is always gratifying," he said.

"Cyril here thinks he's another Oscar Wilde," Sean said.

"Not at all. I'm far more original."

"Come on," Cyn said to Jane. "I'll introduce you to some of the girls. They are bound to be in the music room this hour of the afternoon."

She led Jane along the hall, which seemed endless, to a large room with a wall of tall windows. The afternoon sunlight that streamed through was softened by sheer curtains, which created a gauzy wall of glowing whiteness. In one corner rested a grand piano. The oak floor of the room was not covered by a carpet. Two women danced in the open central area while a third sat in a wooden chair and watched with a critical expression. None of them was older than eighteen.

"Father's nymphs, we call them" Cyn murmured into Jane's ear as they entered.

"I like your hair," one of the dancers said when she caught sight of Jane.

"Sisters, this is Jane Harwood. Jane, meet Cindy, Tara and Pix. I don't remember their last names, but we never use last names here anyway, so what does it matter?"

"Do you dance?" the seated girl named Pix asked.

"No."

The girl came forward and walked around Jane, studying her body. She lifted the hem of Jane's dress and glanced at her legs before Jane could think to object.

"I'm sure you could dance. You have the build for it. But you'd need to strengthen those thighs. I'll help you, if you like."

"That's very kind of you," Jane said.

"We all dance for Father, even Cyn at times, although she doesn't enjoy it."

"It makes my feet hurt," Cyn explained.

"It's almost time for meditation," Pix said. "Can Jane join us?"

"I don't see why not," Cyn said. "Do you want to join them, Jane?"

"Yes, I think so."

"Have you ever meditated before?"

"I've practiced the exercises in Azarial's book."

"Then you know what we're doing. It's an exercise to still and open the mind to higher spiritual influences. Circle, everybody."

The three girls sat on the floor with their legs crossed.

"It's more comfortable if you remove your shoes," Cyn told Jane.

Jane unlaced her travel boots and slid them off, then sat on the bare floor like the others. Cyn stood behind her.

"Since this is your first time, I'm going to guide you," she said. "Close your eyes. Focus on your breathing. Breathe in time with the others. That's it, nice and slow. Now think of the Summerland. It's a land of perpetual sunshine with rolling green hills and wildflowers growing in the grass. The sky is always clear and blue."

Her cool fingers touched Jane on the temples, making her start, but she did not open her eyes. The fingers moved in slow circles as they massaged her temples. The effect was soothing.

"Open your mind. Let your thoughts be still. You are in the Summerland. Feel the grass on your bare feet and the sun on your face. A breeze ruffles the hairs on your bare arms. Now listen. In the distance you hear laughter and music. Someone is having a party. Walk toward the music without opening your eyes."

Jane heard the notes of a fiddle and moved toward it. The sun warmed her cheeks. The tall grass tickled her bare legs. She was filled with a dreaming languor that was indescribably pleasant.

"Now open your eyes," a voice said to her.

She opened her eyes and saw … something. Terror surged in her heart. In an instant it was gone, and she could not remember the image. In its place was the music room. She stood up stiffly with her heart still thudding and looked around. It was empty. Cyn and the three dancers had vanished.

The angle of the light coming through the tall windows had changed. She wondered if she had fallen asleep? How much time had passed? She experienced a moment of irritation when she realized they had just left her on the floor without waking her.

Slipping on her boots, she wandered into the empty hall, then decided to ascend the stair and examine her room. In the upper corridor she passed an elderly servant who eyed her with disapproval.

"My name is Jane Harwood. Could you show me to my bedchamber?"

The old man nodded and turned to walk along the corridor on noiseless feet. He stopped before one of the closed doors.

"Thank you," Jane said dryly.

He turned away before she even finished speaking. Evidently Mrs. Reeves house guests were not well received by the staff, she thought. Not that there was much staff for such a big house.

The room was large, the furniture old, the four-poster bed enormous. The smell of dust hung on the air, as though the room had been very recently swept and aired, and the dust had not yet had a chance to settle. She went to the window. It extended almost from the floor to the ceiling. The drapes were a heavy brocade that had once been red, but had faded over the decades to a kind of rusty brown. She slapped her hand against one side and a shower of dust fell out.

Out on the rear lawn, two young men were playing tennis in a dilapidated tennis court of red clay. She heard laughter faintly through the glass, and realized that it was Teddy and his friend, Sean. The young Irishman threw his racket to one side and jumped lightly over the sagging net, then embraced the other man, who also dropped his racket. They began to kiss. Sean slid one hand down and pressed it between the shorter man legs.

When Jane realized what he was doing, she blushed furiously and turned away. She sat on the side of the bed with her hands folded, not knowing how to feel. Embarrassment and indignation rolled through her by turns. After several minutes she got up and crept toward the window. The tennis court was empty.

She had heard about the doctrine of free love, but this was the first time she had seen an example of it. She found it revolting, yet at the same time strangely intriguing. She realized that she was perspiring. Taking a lace handkerchief from the pocket of her dress, she patted her flushed forehead and cheeks.

Cyn entered the room.

"There you are. I've been looking all over the house for you. We're getting ready to have dinner."

"Do I have time to dress?"

"Don't bother with that old-fashioned custom. Most of us don't dress for dinner. It's come as you are in this house."

She left before Jane could say more.

Jane found a pitcher of fresh water and a basin in the commode. She washed her face and hands, then changed into her simple gray dinner dress. It was one thing not to dress for dinner at home, as an act of rebellion, but quite another to violate social convention in the house of strangers. She had no idea where the dining room might be, but she followed the murmur of conversation and discovered it. The long table that dominated the room could seat a dozen people. There was another smaller table in the corner. Both were set with china and silverware. Steam rose from several platters of sliced pork.

"There she is," Cyn said cheerfully. All eyes turned to Jane. "I saved you a seat."

Jane was amazed by the absence of the formality she had been accustomed to throughout her life. The houseguests sat chatting cheerfully while the elderly servants bustled around preparing the table. Jane searched the faces for Mrs. Reeves but did not find her. Neither was Azarial present. Instead, at the head of the table sat the silent and immobile Miss Voor. Jane took her seat beside Cyn.

The big woman picked up a knife and tapped the water glass by her plate. She kept tapping it until the room was silent. Everyone put the palms of their hands together and pressed them to their foreheads, shutting their eyes. After a moment, Jane imitated the gesture, and heard Cyn speak beside her.

"We of the Rose Circle give thanks to the spirits of Summerland who guide, inspire and animate our lives. Amen."

A chorus of "Amens" ran through the room. Jane opened her eyes. Immediately the diners began to talk and laugh while forking food from the platters onto their plates and passing around bowls. It was a kind of organized chaos. Cyn helped her fill her plate. The slice of pork looked dry, the potato shrivelled, and the heap of green vegetables of no determinable origin, so overcooked were they. The chopped carrots appeared to be unspoiled and the butter in its dish looked wholesome enough. Jane cut her steaming potato and applied butter to it.

"We live like gypsies in this house," Cyn explained. "It's catch as catch can. Don't be afraid to ask for something if you need it – that's the only way you'll ever get it. The servants are half dead, and they don't like us very much. They think we're uncouth, which of course we are. But young Teddy straightened them out. He told them they would have to look after us if they wanted to remain in his grandmother's employ, and most of them stayed on, I think mostly out of loyalty to the old woman."

"Where is Mrs. Reeves?"

"She doesn't eat with us. She takes her meals in her sitting room."

"Does Azarial ever come to the table?"

"Never. He dines alone. Miss Voor acts the part of his familiar daemon and sits at the head of table in his place. But don't be anxious, you will meet him soon enough, when you are properly prepared."

After dinner, as Jane was rising from the table, Cyn took her hand and drew her out of the dining room.

"You must come with me. We're going to have a poetry reading in the library. It will be great fun, it always is."

Jane allowed herself to be led to the library, where people were gathering and positioning themselves on cushions on the worn Persian carpet in a semicircle before a lectern. Cyn pulled Jane to an ancient leather sofa. They sat on it together with their legs curled up.

Cyril James took his place at the lectern. He rapped with his knuckles for silence, glaring around the room until everyone complied, then began to read in French.

> *La sottise, l'erreur, le péché, la lésine*
> *Occupent nos esprits et travaillent nos corps,*
> *Et nous alimentons nos aimables remords,*
> *Comme les mendiants nourrissent leur vermine.*

"What is he reading?" Jane asked.

Cyn listened for a few moments. "I think it's Baudelaire."

On the low table in front of the sofa there was a glass vessel half-filled with liquid. Smoke rising from its tulip-shaped top emitted an unpleasant acrid odor. A long hose lay coiled about it like a serpent. Cyn uncoiled it and put the ivory nozzle on its end to her lips. The liquid in the vessel bubbled. Her eyes opened wider, then half-closed. She extended the hose to Jane.

"Here, you try it."

Jane eyed the vessel uncertainly.

"I've never used tobacco."

Cyn laughed. "It's not tobacco, silly. Go on, try it."

Jane took the nozzle of the hose. "What do I do?"

"You breath in through the little pipe. Try not to cough. Just take a little bit at first."

Jane sucked gently on the tube, and watched the bubbles rise in the glass vessel. She repressed the urge to cough and let the smoke curl out of her nose.

"It's called a hookah," Cyn said, stretching her arms, then folding them behind her head. "It's from Egypt."

They passed the hose back and forth, listening to the French poetry, which Jane with her limited knowledge of French only half-understood. After a time she began to feel light-headed. She giggled, then wondered why.

"What's he saying?" she asked Cyn. The other woman cocked her head and listened for time, then translated.

"I'll plunge my brow, enamoured with voluptuousness, within this darkling ocean of infinitude, or something like that," she said. She listened a little longer. "O fertile weariness; unending lullaby of perfumed lassitude."

Jane leaned her head against the back of the sofa. The library was gently spinning.

"Father wouldn't let me read Baudelaire. He said it was perverse and evil. But he's dead, so he can't stop me."

Cyn leaned over and kissed her on the lips. Jane did not resist.

"You have a new Father now, and he won't forbid you to do anything."

Eventually they left the library. Cyn guided Jane up the stairs to her room and watched her undress for bed.

"There is one thing I need to ask you," Cyn said.

"Ask anything, and you shall receive," Jane told her, spinning on her heel and almost falling before Cyn caught her.

"Are you a virgin?"

"Don't be silly," Jane said, laughing.

Cyn gripped her by the shoulders and made Jane meet her ice-blue gaze.

"I'm serious, Jane. This is important. Are you a virgin?"

Jane focused on her face and blushed. "What a rude question to ask."

"Then you are?'

"Of course I'm a virgin. I'm not married."

Cyn relaxed and released her shoulders. She smiled at Jane.

"You've had too much Turkish delight. Go to bed, Jane. I'll tuck you in."

Obedient as a child, Jane allowed herself to be put to bed. She was asleep before Cyn left the room.

Chapter 5: The Ordeal

Jane felt increasing frustration. She had been living at Briary Place for over two weeks, and had yet to meet with or even see Azarial. Her days were filled with mindless amusements such as croquette, tennis, and modern dance. The nightly poetry readings were beginning to become tiresome, even when they weren't in a foreign language. Almost as an act of self-defence she had begun to sample the intoxicants that were freely available in the house. The hashish she had smoked on her first night was only one of many drugs used by members of the Rose Circle.

"That's the name we use when outsiders ask about us," Cyn had once confided to Jane. "Between ourselves, we call ourselves the Family. We call each other brother and sister, and we call Azarial father."

"You've never called me sister," Jane pointed out.

"That's because you're not one of us yet. First you must finish your training. Then there is an ordeal."

"What ordeal?"

"It's a kind of rite of passage we all went through, as a pledge of loyalty and obedience to Father. Don't fret about it."

"You talk about my training, but I haven't been doing any training."

"You meditate every day, don't you?"

"Yes, but I fall asleep."

"You think you fall asleep?" Cyn said.

"Don't I?"

"When your mind is displaced, your body is host to spirits from the Summerland."

Jane felt a thrill of excitement mingled with fear.

"Have I really been possessed by spirits?"

"Every day since you arrived. You're very mediumistic, Jane. You have a great gift."

The meditation sessions with the young women of the house continued, but there was no more talk of the ordeal, and no sight of Azarial. Jane had wandered alone to the upper level of the house to be by herself and brood. The drug use, and the open sexuality of the others were losing their novelty. She believed that Azarial was ignoring her, and she felt resentment.

Her wandering steps brought her to the closed double doors that led to the west wing of the house. These doors were always kept shut because the west wing had fallen into disrepair, or so she had been told. Curiosity moved her to try the brass handles. They rattled but did not turn downward. It suddenly occurred to her that Azarial might be living in the west wing. It would explain why she had not yet encountered him.

Someone must have the key to the doors, she thought. Probably all the keys were in the keeping of Miss Voor, who ran the household. Her heart sank. There was no hope of getting the key away from that mountain of a woman. Teddy Reeves might have a spare set, she thought, but Teddy was out riding with his friend, Sean O'Conner. It occurred to her that old Mrs. Reeves might know where a spare key to the west wing was kept.

Descending to the first level, she went to the small sitting room where the old women spent most of her time. Mrs. Reeves was in her usual wingback chair before the fireplace. She reminded Jane a little bit of her grandmother, and for a moment she felt a sharp pang of homesickness.

"Mrs. Reeves?"

The old woman, who was nodding to sleep in the chair, jerked awake and looked up at her with cloudy eyes.

"I was curious about the west wing," she began.

""We don't use it," the old woman said with a shake of her head. "Run down. No money to fix it."

"I know, but I was wondering if you would mind if I walked through it, just to see what it is like."

"Please yourself," the other said with a sniff.

"The upstairs doors to the west wing are locked. Do you know where there is a key?"

"Keys? Keys? The old women squinted in thought. "That desk. Top drawer."

Jane opened the left upper drawer of the desk. It contained nothing but yellowed writing paper. The center drawer was empty. The right drawer stuck in its track. Something rattled when she jerked it stiffly open. A ring of antique keys lay on a stack of old copies of the *Atlantic Monthly*. Jane brought the ring back to the old woman.

"Which is the key to the west wing, do you remember?"

Mrs. Reeves waved her away with her hand.

"I don't remember. Take them all and try them, my dear."

Jane concealed the key ring in a pocket of her dress as she left the sitting room. She suspected that if Cyn or Miss Voor learned of what she intended, they would stop her. This might be her one chance to gain access to Azarial and persuade him to teach her.

One after another, she tried the keys on the ring in the double doors. The fifth key, as long as her middle finger and made of black iron, turned stiffly in the lock. She pulled one side open, and with a nervous glance behind her, slipped through and closed it.

She was surprised the floor was so clean. She had expected a layer of dust on the oak boards and the central carpet runner. Someone must sweep it regularly. The upper west wing was not quite as abandoned as she had been led to believe. Hope rose in her heart that Azarial was living in one of these rooms. The first door on her right opened easily.

The room was largely empty. An enormous round carpet occupied the center of the floor, in the middle of which was a small box-like structure about four feet in height that resembled an altar. It was painted black, with arcane symbols on its sides in silver and gold. Jane recognized some of the signs of the zodiac. On its top burned a brass oil lamp with an open flame. Against one wall, a tall wardrobe stood that had also been painted black, but it was undecorated. She opened it, and found that it contained several black robes embroidered with silver thread. In one corner of the wardrobe stood a sword in its leather sheath. A staff leaned beside it. It was divided into sections of different colors.

Jane closed the cabinet and went to a door she judged must lead into the adjoining room. The crystal doorknob refused to turn. Undaunted, she began to try the keys. They made a faint jingle in the silence. She grew nervous, and inserted the keys more and more quickly, causing her to fumble with them. None turned in the lock. She began to try the first key again, intending to make sure doubly sure they did not fit, when the door was abruptly jerked open.

Framed in the opening, and almost filling it, stood Miss Voor in her habitual dress of drab black. The giant woman stared down at Jane, who dropped the ring of keys. It clattered as it struck the floor.

"I didn't know you were in there, Miss Voor," Jane said, trying not to let her voice shake. "I was just having a look around –"

The mute woman moved with astonishing quickness for someone of her size. She bent to snatch the keys from the floor, then continued toward Jane, who stumbled backward. Mrs. Voor's great hand, larger than that of most men, gripped her arm near the shoulder with enough force to make Jane cry out in pain. She continued walking, drawing Jane along with her as easily as if Jane were a small child.

Only when they stood on the landing outside the doors to the west wing did she release Jane.

"How dare you," Jane said. "How dare you lay your hands upon me."

Miss Voor regarded her for a moment. Then, quick as lightning, she slapped Jane across the cheek. The force of the blow knocked Jane to her hands and knees. Her ears rang and her vision blurred. She heard the doors to the west wing slam shut, and when she blinked and looked up, she was alone.

Tears started from her eyes and coursed down her cheeks, one of which was still burning from the slap. Never in her life had she been treated with physical violence, not even as a young child. She did not like the new experience. Standing unsteadily, she wiped her eyes with her handkerchief and descended to the main level, where she met Cyn, who was just entering through the front door.

The other woman's eyes widened when she saw Jane. "What in heaven happened to you? Your cheek is all red."

Jane described the incident, choking back sobs of mingled shame and rage. To her amazement, Cyn only laughed.

"Miss Voor treats us all like naughty children. In her mind you were being disobedient and needed to be disciplined."

"She struck me," Jane said with indignation.

"Hardly that. It was only a slap. It's not as though she used her fist on you."

Jane was speechless at Cyn's apparent indifference to the attack.

"Is this the first time you've ever been slapped?'

Jane nodded.

"That explains why you're so upset. We don't worry about such little things here. Miss Voor is Father's right hand, you know. She is strict, but she is always fair."

"Does Azarial know how she treats his students?"

"Father knows everything."

"Surely he doesn't approve of such behavior."

"You violated his wishes, Jane. You went where you were forbidden."

"No one forbade me to explore the west wing."

"The doors were locked. What did you think locked doors meant?"

Jane felt her face burning with her anger. "I'm leaving. I'll go upstairs and pack my bags."

Cyn caught her by the arm.

"You can't leave now. Today is the day of your ordeal. Once you pass through that you can talk to Father and complain about Miss Voor, if you want."

"Father will see me?" Jane asked. She hesitated.

"Yes, we all talk to Father. After your ordeal you'll be one of the Family. He will want to see you."

"When is this ordeal to take place?"

"Right now. I was just coming in to fetch you for it. Everyone's waiting for you at the summer house."

Jane was torn between her outrage and shame at being struck in the face, and her intense desire to see Azarial again. Once she stood in his presence and spoke to him, she felt inwardly that everything would be all right. She longed to hear the power of his voice soothing and instructing her.

"We all went through it," Cyn urged. "It's just a little school girl hazing, to make you feel like one of us. What does one slap in the face matter in the greater scheme of things?"

Jane sighed in resignation. "Do I need to change my dress?"

"No, what you are wearing is fine. Hurry along with me."

They went outside and walked across the unkempt lawn with quick strides to the bank of the pond where the summer house stood. It was a timber-frame structure of eight sides, all of them having window screens to let in the light and exclude insects. Members of the Family were gathered inside. Standing with them was the Boston medium Leda French and her mouse-like husband, Walter.

"This is a great day for you, Jane," she said in her booming voice as Jane and Cyn entered the summer house. "You must be so excited. Today you become one of our circle."

"What am I to do?" Jane asked.

"You need only listen to instructions, do as you are told, and not become afraid."

"Don't be shocked, dear Jane," Cyn whispered in her ear. "It's really not so bad, and it's over very quickly."

"You must bare yourself to the waist," Mrs. French told her.

Jane stared at her, wondering if she had heard rightly.

"Don't be a prude, Jane," Cyril James said in a tired voice. "You know what goes on in this house. We've all seen nipples before, believe me."

Cyn began to unbutton Jane's dress. Jane started to resist, but a voice deep in her mind told her to relax and let it happen. In moments the upper part of her dress and her white cotton chemise hung from her hips. The breeze felt cool on her bare breasts and made them dimple with goose bumps. She felt her face burning with embarrassment. She kept her gaze directed straight ahead, not really seeing what was in front of her but feeling everything.

"Now you must repeat after me, line for line," Cyril said, unrolling a parchment scroll in his hands. He read, "I, Jane Harwood, give my solemn oath of fealty to the Rose Circle, and swear that I shall never violate its laws or customs, nor betray the trust of my brothers and sisters under the rose."

Jane repeated in a toneless voice each line as it was spoken. She felt herself strangely detached from the ceremony. Her shame at being half-naked still burned, but it was locked somewhere inside her where it was no longer visible.

"Good girl," Cyril said. "Now you must face your ordeal, and demonstrate your courage. Come forward."

Jane's hands were taken on either side and raised. Soft sashes were tied around her wrists by Pix and Tara, and her arms spread and elevated above her head as the sashes were pulled tight over the exposed roof beams of the summer house. They stepped back from her, their faces solemn. Cyn nodded her silent encouragement. Jane felt someone approach behind her and wondered if it was Azarial. The thought gave her courage.

Something slashed across her back with a loud crack, and her body bent forward like a drawn bow. She cried out and turned her head. Miss Voor stood behind her, expressionless. In her hand was a kind of whip with a short, thick handle that had many strips of leather dangling from its end.

Again the whip slashed across her back, and she screamed, struggling to pull her hands out of the sashes. Her struggles made no difference. The fall of the leather strips across her back was as relentless as a metronome. Again and again the pain lashed through her, until here entire body tingled with a strange heat that was almost pleasurable. She began to breathe in rhythm with the lashes, her breasts heaving, her nipples hard little spikes that dripped with sweat.

As suddenly as it began, it was over. Gentle hands untied her wrists and caught her before she collapsed. They guided her to a bench and sponged the blood from her back.

"You see, Jane, it really wasn't so bad," Cyn told her.

"She was well prepared," Jane heard Mrs. French say behind her.

"She takes the training well," Cyril James said. "Her mind is quite receptive."

"Father will be pleased."

"Will I meet Father now?" Jane asked in a weak voice.

"Soon, my dear," Mrs. French told her, leaning so close Jane smelled peppermint on her breath. "Very soon."

Chapter 6: The Pact

Jane's back healed quickly. It was mostly red welts that crisscrossed her milk-white skin. Here and there, the leather tassels of the whip had broken the skin and caused blood to run down, giving the appearance of more damage than actually existed. She lay in her room for a day, attended to by Cyn, than quickly recovered her strength.

Three days after the ordeal, Jane was walking with Cyn in the shade of the trees that bordered the drive when she noticed a man lurking at the wrought-iron gate. At first she did not recognize him, but there was something familiar in the way he moved. She went toward the gate with Cyn following behind her.

"Robert?"

"Jane," he said. "It is you. I wasn't sure, you were so far away."

"What are you doing here?"

"I've been searching for you. Your mother is half-mad with worry. She asked me to find you."

He was greatly changed from the young man she had once promised to marry. He was unshaven and his hair was dishevelled. He was thinner than she remembered, and there was a wildness in his eyes.

"How did you find me?"

He tried to laugh, but failed, and took something from his pocket. "I had that tintype you gave me a year ago. Do you remember it? I went around Boston, showing it to everyone I met in the street. I must have shown it to thousands of people. A grocery delivery man thought he recognized you from his deliveries at this house. And here you are."

"Jane stared at the small portrait of herself. It no longer resembled her. The change was more than just her hairstyle and choice of dress. It was her expression, the set of her mouth, the light in her eyes. She was more knowing now, more serious but also more mystical. It was like looking at a portrait of herself from early childhood. She felt no connection with it.

"You needn't have come, Robert. You should not have come. I am perfectly well, as you can see."

He stared at her with red-rimmed eyes. Jane wondered when last he had slept, or had a decent meal.

"I've come to take you home, Jane. Your mother needs you. She hasn't been the same since you left. She calls out to you in her sleep."

He reached through the iron bars of the gate. Jane took a step backward. Standing behind her, Cyn put her hands on Jane's shoulders.

"Is this your former fiancé?" she asked, amusement in her voice.

"Yes."

"Go away, silly man," Cyn said. "Jane belongs with us now."

"Jane, do these people have some hold over you? In town they said this house is filled with anarchists and dope fiends. Is that true?"

Jane squared her shoulders and hardened her feelings. "Tell Mother that I am well and that I am happy. This is where I want to be."

"Jane, if you could let me in so that we could talk about this."

"That would change nothing, Robert. I'm not as I was when you knew me. I've moved on to a higher spiritual plane."

"These demons have twisted your mind," he said with sudden savagery. "I'll get the police. Your mother will have you removed for your own well being."

"Call the police," Cyn told him. "Jane is here because she wants to be here. She is a guest of the Reeves, as I am."

"I can't talk to you any longer, Robert. This is an important time in my life. I must focus my spiritual energies on what lies in store for me," Jane said.

"Lies in store for you?" he repeated. "What do you mean? What are they going to do to you?"

"No more, Robert. Please just go. Tell Mother I am happy here. Go now, please."

Cyn gently pulled her away from the gate and put one arm around her shoulders, leading her up the gravel drive toward the house. When Jane looked back, Robert was still there.

"Do you love him?" Cyn asked.

"I thought I did, once. Not anymore."

"Then think no more about him. He is of your past. We are your future."

Cyril James met them at the front door of the house. His eyes shone with enthusiasm.

"Father has called for you."

Jane's heart began to race. "When?"

"Now. I'm to take you up to him."

"But I should change my dress."

"There's no time."

"Go with Cyril," Cyn said. "We'll talk after the meeting."

They passed Miss Voor going up the stairs. The big woman stopped and stared at them.

"I'm to see Father," Jane blurted out in her excitement.

Miss Voor's expression did not change. She turned away and continued down the stair.

Jane approached the doors of the west wing, her legs trembling with each step. Both sides of the doors stood wide open.

"Remember what I've told you," Cyril murmured. "Don't speak until Father addresses you, and respond briefly to his questions. If he wants your conversation, he will invite it – otherwise, remain silent. Be respectful."

They stopped at the opened doors.

"Here I must leave you, Sister. I know you won't disgrace yourself. You are part of our Family now, and always."

Jane peered nervously down the shadowy corridor.

"Go through the second door on the right. Wait for his summons. What passes between you and Father is for you alone. Do not speak of it afterwards."

"I'm ready," she said, and walked forward into the west wing.

Her steps were measured. She paused at the second door and turned, but Cyril was already gone. Opening it, she entered and found a small sitting room with several comfortable chairs. She sat in one and waited. Minutes passed.

On both side walls of the room were doors. She already knew what lay behind one of them. It was the room with the altar. From the door on the other side came the low murmur of a voice. It seemed to be chanting, or praying. The voice fell silent. After several minutes, Jane heard the single clear chime of a brass bell.

She sat, listening. Was that her signal to enter the other room? She waited, but no other sounds came through the door. At last she went to the door, and with thudding heart put her hand on its crystal knob and opened it.

The air in the room beyond was laden with the heavy odor of rose petals. The scent was so strong, it was almost sickening in its sweetness. Incense smouldered in a brass censor that hung on three brass chains from the ceiling. The rising smoke coiled and undulated in a beam of afternoon sunlight slanting through the window.

Azarial sat cross-legged on a pile of brightly colored silk cushions. He was smoking a clay pipe with a long, curved stem. Taking the end from his lips, he used it to point at her.

"Enter."

He spoke softly, but his voice filled the room.

Jane came forward across the red Persian carpet until she was in the center.

"Sit."

She glanced around for a chair, and not seeing any, sat down with her legs crossed on the carpet.

"You are a seeker of truth, Jane," he said languidly after a long pause. "I saw that in you the first time we met. That is why I invited you here."

His eyelids were heavy and half-closed. When he drew smoke from the pipe, his cheeks hollowed, showing the outlines of the bones of his skull. Under the sickly-sweet smell of the rose incense was a sharper, more acrid tang that Jane did not recognize. She wondered if it came from the pipe.

"You have questions."

"Yes."

"Ask."

Jane felt a moment of panic. She had many times imagined this meeting, but had not rehearsed what she would say when it occurred.

"What is the purpose of the Rose Circle?"

He drew smoke from the pipe and held it, then released it slowly between his thin lips.

"We are a bridge between this life and the next. We facilitate the union of the living with those who exist beyond this realm."

"Am I to be trained to become a medium?"

He smiled. "My dear child, you already are one."

"I don't understand."

"Over the past several weeks you have given us most interesting communications from the other side."

She shook her head, frowning in puzzlement.

He set his pipe into a holder on a small round table beside the cushions and stood effortlessly. With four quick strides he came to her. She began to get up, but he put a hand on her shoulder. Sitting in front of her so that their knees almost touched, he supported her chin in his hand and studied her face. Jane felt a thrill flash along her nerves at the touch, and a tingle between her thighs.

Sitting so near to him, she felt his vitality radiate against her like a physical force. She wondered if it was his aura she sensed. He put his hands to the sides of her face and rubbed her temples with his fingertips.

"What are you doing?" she asked nervously.

"Verifying your conditioning."

He spoke a word. She saw his lips move but heard nothing. There was a strange lapse in her thinking. She blinked and saw with astonishment that he was once again across the room, seated on the cushions.

"How did you –"

"You are ready to become fully united with us, Jane. Know now that you have been chosen for a great honor. The Summerland has four gates, which are set in watchtowers at the corners of our world. Our work has succeeded in opening the western gate, but only a crack, only wide enough for the occasional passage of a spirit, and only for brief minutes. You will help us open all four gates wide, so that the beings of the other planes may come through as they wish, without hindrance."

"How is it that I can help you?"

"You must participate in a special ceremony. Indeed, you must become its central focus. I swear to you that we will not physically harm you, but the ritual requires submission and obedience on your part."

Jane's thoughts raced. Was she to be beaten again? The prospect terrified her, yet at the same time she felt strangely excited by it.

"Am I to be whipped?"

"No. That ordeal is passed. You have within you a pure flame that must be kindled, and by its light the chains and locks will melt from the gates, and they will swing wide. Nothing unnatural will be done to you, on that you have my word."

"Very well. I will participate in the ceremony."

His faded-blue eyes opened wide, and seemed to flash fire. Then they rolled up in his head so that only the whites showed.

"You have chosen wisely," said a female voice from his lips. "For this sacrifice you will be rewarded by the hosts of the blessed."

The voice was a deep contralto. Jane realized it was the same voice that had spoken from him in Edwards Hall.

"Who are you?"

"I am Azarial, he is Azarial, we are Azarial." He spread his arms. "This is only a vessel through which I am enabled to interact with your world. But soon that will change. My brothers and sisters will fill your world with our brightness, which is like unto the radiant flame of the Morning Star. Then you will receive our wisdom, as you did long ago when the world was young."

"I don't understand."

"Understanding will come to you, in time."

He stood straight up simply by straightening his legs and went to a table against a wall.

Come here, Sister Jane."

She got up stiffly and went to him. He showed her a sheet of paper with writing on it.

"This is a formal declaration that you participate in our ceremony of your own free will, and that no coercion has been used on you. Will you sign it?"

She took the paper and read the flowing script, wondering why such a written declaration was necessary. Did Azarial intend to show it to her mother, or to the police should they be sent looking for her?

"Time is pressing, child. I have work to do," he said in his female voice. "We need you, Jane. We cannot proceed without you."

She accepted the fountain pen he offered to her and signed at the bottom of the document.

"Now, your seal," the spirit said.

171

Azarael took her right hand and quickly cut the ball of her thumb with a pen knife. She made an involuntary sound of surprise and tried to draw back her hand, but the spirit held her wrist in a grip that was like a steel vise. A drop of blood beaded up from the tiny wound.

"Press your thumb on the paper next to your signature," Azarael told her. "I cannot do it for you."

The spirit released her wrist and Jane rubbed it. She hesitated.

Azarael's eyes returned to normal. His expression was stern.

"If you do not do this, you will be expelled from the Rose Circle," he said in his male voice.

Still she hesitated.

"You have been chosen, Jane. You alone, from all the women of the world. This is your destiny. Do not cast it away."

Biting her lower lip, she pressed her thumb to the paper and peeled it off, leaving her thumb print clearly defined in blood.

He took the paper, scanned it over, and smiled.

"One more thing, at some point in the future you must write to your mother and set her mind at ease. Tell her that you are happy here."

"I will do so, Azarial."

"In this letter you should ask her to send you money on a weekly basis to defray your expenses. Tell her you need it to buy food and clothing."

"But I lack for nothing."

He smiled at her. "The expenses of the Rose Circle are great. Every member must contribute whatever he or she can."

"Of course, I understand."

"Leave me now," he said, turning away. "We will talk again, and at greater length, after the ceremony."

"When is the ceremony to take place?"

"This very night." His faced her, and his expression frightened her with its sheer intensity. "Together we shall make a new world upon the ashes of the old. Now go, and tell no one what has passed between us."

Chapter 7: The Ceremony

That evening the three nymphs, Cindy, Tara and Pix, came to her room with the hooded robe she was to wear for the ceremony. It was made of silk, black on the outside with a blood-red lining.

"What am I to wear under it?" Jane asked as she ran the smooth cloth between her fingers.

"Nothing," Tara said.

"Nothing at all?"

"Nothing. The esoteric energies flowing along the surface of your skin must be unimpeded."

"What about my feet?"

"Nothing."

They helped her undress. She stood naked and shivering in the cool night air. The fire in the bedroom fireplace had burned so low, it was nearly out. The three girls slipped her arms through the loose sleeves of the robe and closed it in front. Its hem almost touched the floor.

"Where is the ceremony to take place?" she asked.

"In the chapel," Tara said.

Briary Place had a detached family chapel just behind the house that had not been used for decades. Shortly after her arrival, Jane had investigated it, and had found it of little interest. The religious artefacts had been stripped out. All that remained was the altar under a stained glass window that depicted the crucifixion of Christ.

"You must walk to the chapel along the gravel path on your bare feet. It is important that you do not flinch or cry out. Have faith. The stones will not cut you. Father will protect you."

"I'm not afraid," Jane murmured. But this was not entirely true.

The wait for the hour of the ceremony was excruciating for Jane. Cyn came and sat beside her on her bed, holding her hand. She wore a long white dress.

"It won't be long," she said. "Father has to wait for the auspicious astrological hour to arrive before we begin."

"What is the ceremony about?" Jane asked. "Can't you tell me?"

"I'm forbidden to tell you. It is our highest mystery, and you must react to it as it takes place, without forewarning. But there is no need to fear."

"Have you taken part in it before?"

Cyn laughed. "Three years ago, I was wearing the same robe that you wear tonight. I was just as nervous as you are, Jane, even though the ritual I participated in was not nearly as important as the one we will perform tonight. Have faith in Father."

Jane's gaze fell upon Cyn's hand as it gave her own a reassuring squeeze.

"You never did tell me how you lost your little finger."

"You are so intuitive, Jane. That's why Father has a special interest in you. I think you are going to become his favorite."

"Isn't Miss Voor his favorite?"

"No, she's more like a servant." Cyn paused for a moment. "I am his favorite."

"Then you must remain so. I have no wish to steal his favor from you."

"I know that. But Father will favor whomever he chooses, and he has taken an interest in you, Jane. He sees something in you."

These words excited Jane on a deep level, but she tried not to show it.

Teddy Reeves appeared at the open door of the bedchamber. He wore a gray robe with a hood that hung down his back.

"Everything is ready," he said with his boyish grin.

The three nymphs met them at the rear door of the house as they emerged into the chill night air. Each wore a white dress and carried a white candle. Their flames fluttered, although there was almost no breeze. Teddy left them and ran on ahead to the chapel, through the open door of which light glowed. Tara passed a candle to Cyn and lit it with her own. The four young women surrounded Jane, two on each side, as they walked slowly along the gravel path toward the chapel.

At first the sharp gravel bruised Jane's bare feet. She had to bite her lip to keep from whimpering. Then the soles of her feet became numb and she no longer felt the stones.

The interior of the chapel blazed with the light of dozens of candles. Incense smoke rose from a charcoal brazier on a tripod. She recognized the scent of frankincense. All the members of the Family were there, standing around the wooden altar. On its surface rested a silver chalice and a knife. The women wore the same white dresses, the men, matching gray robes save for Azarial, who was dressed in a black robe similar to the one that covered Jane. He stood alone behind the altar, looking grim and imposing to Jane's eyes. She noticed that Miss Voor was absent, and wondered if the big woman had some role to play later in the course of the ceremony.

"We gather here, on this auspicious hour, to receive this woman, Jane Harwood, into our Family, and to present her to our god, who is ever-hungry for worship," Azarial said in his deep voice.

They all knelt on the marble floor. Jane hesitated, then did the same. The polished marble was cold beneath her knees. Azarael continued to stand. He began to chant words in a strange language Jane had never heard before. She knew it was not Latin, nor did it sound like Greek or Hebrew, but what it might be she could not guess. At intervals, the kneeling worshipers made brief responses in the same language.

Azarial abruptly stopped speaking. He took up the chalice in one hand and the knife in the other and raised both high above his head.

"Let us make our offerings to our god, that his hunger may be appeased for this night, lest he come for one of us and take that one away with him, although surely it would be an honor to be so chosen."

He set the chalice back on the altar and used the knife to cut his left forearm, then allowed a trickle of blood to drip into the chalice. One by one, the worshipers kneeling around the altar stood, came forward, and received the knife to cut themselves on the forearm. Jane watched in mounting apprehension, wondering if she would be expected to do the same. She had never deliberately cut herself, and did not know if she was capable of such an act. Perhaps Father would do it for her, she thought, and this hope made her feel better.

He met her gaze, as though aware that she was thinking of him. "Arise, my child. It is time for your sacrifice."

Jane stood up on stiff legs and approached the altar. Nervously, she took the blood-stained knife. When she reached for the chalice, Azarial drew it away from her.

"You initial sacrifice to the god is not blood, but must be something greater."

"I don't understand," she said in a small voice, her throat dry.

"Each of us had made a sacrifice from our body. Show her, Sister Cyn."

Cyn held up her left hand with its four fingers.

"Most choose the small toe as their sacrifice, or the little finger, but the choice is yours, Sister."

Fear mingled with revulsion rose like a fountain within Jane. Azarial wanted her to willingly mutilate herself. Every instinct inside her revolted against the thought. She looked from side to side, seeking an opening in the circle of worshippers that she could dart through.

Azarial reached across the altar and took her head between his large hands. He spoke a single word that she somehow failed to hear. Instantly, her fear vanished, replaced by a kind of numbness.

"Choose," he said.

Jane watched herself from above, as though her consciousness has left her body and floated high in the chaple dome. She saw her right hand raise the bloody knife to her face. Her left hand brushed away her hair and grasped her left ear. With a single stroke she cut off her ear and held it out. It dripped scarlet droplets across the altar top.

"Place your sacrifice in the chalice," Azarial said.

She watched her left hand drop the severed ear into the silver chalice, which was half-filled with blood. Then her body stepped back into the ring of worshippers and knelt. Once more she found herself inside her own flesh. Blood trickled wetly down the left side of her neck, but it seemed unimportant, like the blood of another person.

One by one, the members of the Rose Circle stood and came forward to receive the sacrament of their mingled blood. Azarial touched the chalice to their lips and they sipped the dark ichor. When Jane's turn came, she passively did as the others had done. The blood had a metallic taste on her tongue, but her stomach did not revolt. After all had drunk, Azarial reached into the chalice and took out her bloody ear. He recited several words in the language he had used earlier and placed the ear into his mouth. He began to chew. Jane heard the cartilage in her ear crunch between his teeth. Then he swallowed.

"Position her body on the alter," he said with bloody lips.

Cyn and Tara approached Jane from one side, Teddy and Cyril from the other. They took her by the arms and drew her toward the altar. Azarial removed the chalice and knife. It was only when they began to bend Jane back across the altar top that she found the power to resist.

"What are you doing?" she protested weakly.

"Don't resist," Cyn murmured into her bloody ear hole. "It will all be over in a few minutes."

The highest sacrifice to our nameless god must be pure and undefiled," Azarial said. "Behold, a young virgin who has never known a man. We offer her to you, Dark One. Enter me as I enter her. Ravish me as I ravish her. Make one spirit with me as I unite my flesh to hers."

Jane fought with increasing desperation, but all four of her limbs were held. She was bent onto her back upon the altar so that her legs hung over its side at the knees and her arms were spread wide. Azarial stepped between her thighs as the kneeling members of the circle raised their arms and began to chant barbarous words that seemed to resonate and come alive on the air. Azarial gripped the front of Jane's robe and swept it apart, exposing her white skin to the chillness and the candlelight. She thrashed her head from side to side but could not free her limbs. Her hair stuck to the altar where the blood from her wound pooled on its surface.

With a dramatic gesture Azarial tore his own robe apart, framing his naked body in the scarlet of its lining. His sexual organ was fully erect. Jane had never seen anything like it before. Her mother had told her about the way men and woman couple to produce children, but the reality of this fleshy limb, like some deformed third leg, swollen with purple blood and dripping from its end, terrified and revolted her. It bobbed up and down as he leaned forward across the altar, supporting himself on his hands. His face hung above hers, and his faded blue eyes burned down into her very soul.

Then the pain came. It got worse, and worse, until she began to scream. Something tore inside her. The thing between his legs filled her in a way that felt unnatural. He began to move, thrusting slowly but with great force so that each thrust rocked her entire body. Sweat dripped from his face into her eyes and mouth. It seemed to go on for hours, the slow, brutal pounding of that naked club inside her belly. The chants of the circle filled her ears and maddened her.

Just as she began to think that the worst of the pain might be over, his face, so close above hers, began to change. It became broader, more brutal, the cheekbones wider, the chin more blunt. His black hair seemed to grow longer and hung down to brush her lips and nose. His wildly staring eyes sank in their sockets and darkened to black. Then she was looking into the serpent-like eyes of Miss Voor, who smiled when she saw recognition in Jane's face. It was the first time Jane had ever seen her smile.

Jane felt something hot gush between her legs, like a splash of fresh blood from an open wound. Miss Voor threw back her massive head and bellowed like a bull. It shook the walls of the chapel and made the flames of the candles flutter.

"She comes!" Cyril James shouted in a high-pitched, hysterical shriek.

The chanting of the circle reached a climax and ceased.

Lightning flashed in the tall window behind the altar, illuminating the figure of Christ on the cross. Looking past the shoulder of Miss Voor, Jane's eyes met those of the stained glass image. They gazed into her very heart with a sorrowful expression. An instant later a clap of thunder shook the very foundations of the chapel. Miss Voor's head exploded, spraying Jane's face with fragments of brain tissue and bits of bone. Screams erupted from the circle of worshippers. Jane heard gunshots, but the weight of the corpse kept her pinned to the altar. The screams and patter of naked, running feet diminished to silence.

The corpse moved upon her. She screamed, and could not stop screaming. Something pulled the dead flesh away. It fell to the marble floor with a wet sound, like a leather bag filled with offal. A man's face leaned over hers.

"Jane, darling, your safe now. He can't hurt you anymore. I've killed him."

She continued to scream, over and over, but the screams became weak until they could barely be heard. He pressed his fingertips to her blood-smeared lips.

"What have they done to you, my poor darling."

Her eyes focused on his face. A spark of recognition kindled in their gray depths.

"I am yours," she said. "Forever and a day, yours."

He hugged her close. Into his ear she whispered, "Azarial."

PUBLICATION HISTORY

Stories original to this collection: "Introduction," "Fingernails," "Found Art," "Janus," "Tongue of the Bell," "Dream A Little Dream of Me," "False Image," "The Ivory Box," "A Leaf from the Cottonian Genesis," "Future Indefinite," "What Is Happening," "The Seed of Vass," and "The Rose Circle."

Previously published stories: "Going to See Mr. Winters" Prize Winner, 1978 Nova Scotia Writing Competition, hosted by Writers' Federation of Nova Scotia. Published in Alpha, Acadia University Students' Union magazine, Fall 1978 issue. "The Glenn of the Green Women" Original version of this story published by Black Cat Mystery Magazine (vol. 1, issue no. 3) in 1981. "Cruising" was published in Twilight Zone Magazine, Sept. 1982 issue. Subsequently republished in the magazine's anthology Night Cry (Summer, 1985). "The Nail" was published in Weird Fiction Review (Fall, 2014).

ABOUT THE AUTHOR

DONALD TYSON has been writing about strange and uncanny things for four decades, both in the form of fiction and nonfiction. He is the author of the collection of stories, *The Skinless Face and Other Horrors* (Weird House, 2020), as well as the seminal novel *Alhazred* (Llewellyn, 2006), a collection of stories detailing Alhazred's adventures as a young man, *Tales of Alhazred* (Dark Renaissance Books, 2015) and a novel concerning Alhazred's quest for a fabled magic talisman, *The Red Stone of Jubbah* (Weird House, 2020). He lives with his wife, Jenny, in a farm house in rural Cape Breton, on the tip of the province of Nova Scotia, Canada.

ABOUT THE ARITIST

Steeped in the enthralling fantasy and science-fiction illustrations of the 1960s, '70s, and '80s, artist and illustrator **K.L. TURNER** brings a bit of old-school painterly style to today's methods. With more than 30 years of experience in the arts, he expertly brings an expressionistic style into his illustrations to create compelling works which captivate and draw the viewer in. His works are found in media and galleries around the world, and celebrated in pop culture. A versatile creative type, Turner is also accomplished in the mediums of photography, sculpture, and the fine arts. Choosing to live and work on the beautiful front range of the Colorado Rocky Mountains where he was born and raised, he continues to derive inspiration from nature as well as cultural influences both at home and in his travels.